THE TROUBLE WITH #9

PIPER RAYNE

Cover Design: By Hang Le

1st Line Editor: Joy Editing

2nd Line Editor: My Brother's Editor

Proofreader: My Brother's Editor

About The Trouble with #9

Trouble.

One word that comes to mind when someone talks about me. I like to think of it as protection, watching out for the ones I love. But now I'm spending more time in the penalty box than on the ice and the team owner isn't happy.

Finding myself across the room from the hot therapist I kissed on New Year's Eve only makes me push my problems down further. I want couch time with her but not the kind she's used to.

I decide to lie to her just to finish off my therapy so I can do what I really want—date her—even if she says she doesn't date hockey players. Just when my therapy sessions are up and I've made some headway with Paisley, it's my parents who throw another wrench in my plans.

If I abide by my parent's wishes to marry the one they've chosen, I'll lose Paisley forever. But if I go against my parents, I'm failing my deceased best friend all over again.

The
Trouble
with # 9

CHAPTER 1

Maksim

"Drake! Petrov!" Coach yells as I skate off the ice after practice, alongside my best friend and our center, Aiden Drake. "Get to the psychologist today and make an appointment. I'm trying to win us a championship and you two can't do one simple thing? Gerhardt's on my ass and I want him off it, you understand me?"

"Already done, Coach. I'm meeting with her right now," Aiden says.

Coach nods and glares at me.

"I don't need therapy," I say.

"Gerhardt says everyone. What makes you so goddamn special?"

My teammates snicker as they pass by.

"I'm Russian, Coach, we don't do the whole 'up in our feelings' shit." I'm being upfront and honest, but instead of understanding, he gives me a look of disgust.

"I don't care if you tell her you believe in fucking unicorns and gold pots at the end of the rainbow. Go to that office and sit down in a chair across from her for one hour." He disappears into his office and slams the door.

"What's the problem?" Aiden asks. "It's not a big deal.

Just tell her your game is good. That you're fucking perfect." He winks and laughs.

I'm not going to admit to anyone that I kissed the therapist, Paisley Pearce, on New Year's Eve. At the time, I had no idea she was going to be our team therapist. But damn, sometimes late at night, I think back on that kiss, and I wonder what if. But there's no changing it, so I need to forget that kiss. The team owner, Carl Gerhardt, wants all the Florida Fury hockey players to go to therapy because he believes it will help us with our game.

"You know this is your fault, right?" I say to Aiden as we reach the locker room, finally realizing who I can blame for this situation.

"My fault?" He takes off his pads.

I sit and unlace my skates. "If it wasn't for your little drought, Gerhardt wouldn't have felt the need to bring someone in."

"Therapy didn't get me out of my slump. Saige did."

Saige is Aiden's girlfriend. They met on New Year's Eve too, but instead of a kiss, he got a drink in the face at midnight.

"Speaking of," he says and picks up his phone, hammering out a text to someone.

"Maybe Saige was your lucky charm, but Gerhardt made those plans before you started scoring again, and now I'm stuck having to sit in some claustrophobic office while that woman stares at me, waiting to fix me."

I don't mention that having Paisley's eyes on me will probably only make me want to make a move again. Which I can't since we'll be under the patient/client umbrella. I don't know Paisley well, but I know enough to know she'd have an issue with it.

"Sorry, man." He doesn't sound apologetic. What does he care? The guy's been on cloud fucking nine since he and Saige became exclusive. "Did I tell you I sent a moving truck to Saige's place? She's moving in with me today."

Knowing Aiden, he didn't even ask, but I'm fairly sure Saige won't object anyway.

"Peachy," I say, and continue to undress so I can shower and change.

Aiden finishes undressing before me and wraps a towel around his waist to head to the showers.

I follow a minute later. "I'm not joking, Aid, get me the fuck out of this."

He laughs, washing his hair. "Why do you think I can do that?"

"Talk to Gerhardt. You're his little pet. Tell him I'm meant to stay angry if he wants me to be the enforcer I am."

How does Gerhardt think I can remain the policeman of this team by slamming opponents into the boards and starting fights with opposing players who try dirty moves on our best guys if I'm all up in my feelings? I'm in the penalty box all the time because I'm the one who lets the other team know not to fuck with us. If they do, they know I'm coming for them. If Paisley gets me to open up and put all my shit out on the table, I might turn soft and lose my hockey career.

"You're making a way bigger deal out of this than it is. Just go for one visit and make Gerhardt happy."

"Hell no. And if it's such a big deal, why are you just going now?" I shampoo my blond hair and allow the warm water to spray down my back.

"I had more important things to take care of." Aiden winks.

He's talking about Saige and I'm this close to ewwing like a seventh grader walking in on his parents banging.

He turns off his water and wraps a towel around

himself. "I'll make you a bet. If I win the bet, then you go to one session right now. You can tag along with me. If I lose, I'll talk to Gerhardt on your behalf."

I narrow my eyes. "What's the bet?"

Aiden's notorious for making bets that are to his advantage, so I'm skeptical. We walk out of the shower room and find Tweetie going through a box of hockey power pack player cards.

"Let's make it easy. Tweet! Toss one over." Aiden holds up his hands.

Tweetie throws a pack to Aiden.

Aiden holds it up in front of me. "If one of our cards is in this pack, that's the winner. If not, we play wars."

"That's just based on luck, man. Give me a skills competition to make this interesting."

"Take it or leave it." He shrugs.

I groan and sit on the bench. "Your cards are probably in these things two for one of mine."

He laughs because he knows I'm right. But the chance that either one of ours is in those packs of cards has to be slim to none.

"Fine." I roll my head in a circle to relieve the stress making my neck muscles tight.

Aiden rips open the pack, and all of our teammates gather round. I'm just thankful Ford's not here since he had to go up to New York to figure out some stuff with his new baby mama. I'd never hear the end of it if I lose and he was here to witness.

Aiden flips through the cards, my breath stuck in my throat the entire time. The thought of sitting in a chair across from Paisley and her wanting to know everything about me and my past gives me anxiety.

His wicked smile makes my chest tighten until Aiden laughs. "Neither of us made the cut."

"Thank fuck," I murmur.

Tweetie grabs the cards and shuffles them. "Okay, guys. You each get five."

He doles out hockey player cards to each of us. The whole point of war with hockey cards is to have the best of whatever category is named.

I stare at my cards, happy that I got a good mix.

Tweetie clears his throat. "Who has the most goals scored in a season?"

Aiden and I thumb through our cards, reading stats of the players.

Aiden slams his on the bench and Tweetie picks it up. "Maksim, you got anything better than forty-six?"

I shake my head and my jaw clenches. Aiden laughs like I knew he would.

"Don't worry, big guy, best of five." Tweetie pats me on the shoulder.

"Who's got the shortest player?" someone calls.

We both go through our cards. I slam one on the bench and Tweetie picks it up.

"Got anything shorter than five-nine?" Tweetie asks Aiden.

He groans.

"Hell yeah," I say.

"Long way to go," Aiden says.

Next, they do draft year, which Aiden wins.

"One more," Tweetie says to Aiden like maybe he wants him to win.

I scowl at Tweetie.

"Who has the youngest player?" another teammate calls.

The two of us scramble. I win that one, which ties us. Aiden stares me down with a cocky smirk.

"Most assists," Tweetie says.

Aiden slams his down right away. Tweetie picks it up and laughs his ass off, revealing to everyone that it's him.

"I'd say this is one good-ass-looking player," Tweetie says. "No way you have a card that beats me on assists."

Tweetie's our left winger and passes that puck to Aiden all the fucking time. Still, I search my cards with a little hope. I shake my head in defeat. Fuck.

"Aiden's the winner!" Tweetie holds up Aiden's arm as though he just won the Cup.

"Thanks, guys. Looks like you're coming with me." He smiles brightly.

We leave the locker room and head up to the executive offices.

Aiden clasps my shoulder and squeezes. "Relax, man, this is nothing. Say whatever you want. You don't have to actually be looking for therapy."

I nod, and we enter the office that's been set aside for Paisley. Since Aiden said he'll go in first, I sit and grab a magazine off the table in front of me.

Aiden takes a seat next to me. "I'm so damn excited for Saige to move in." His knee bounces up and down.

"That's awesome, man." I flip through a *Better Homes & Gardens* magazine. "Is she trying to introduce us to other interests?" I hold up the magazine. "I mean, I'm not taking up gardening to Zen myself out or whatever the hell it's called."

"Try to be positive," he says. "Maybe it'll be a one-and-done session."

Aiden gets called in, and right after the door shuts, Gerhardt walks by the glass office door. He stops for a moment, smiles when he sees me, and carries on his way.

Fuck, that annoys the shit out of me. Not that I don't want to please my boss. I do. Hell, it'd suck to get traded at this point in my career, but the stubborn side of me hates bowing down to the man.

I lower my chin and read about the color patterns popular this spring. Seriously, she needs better reading material if she plans on being a fixture to the team. The guys aren't gonna want to read this shit.

The door to the office opens about fifteen minutes later, and Aiden leaves it propped open for me to step through. He winks and slaps me on the back while we trade places. I sit my ass on the couch across from Paisley, pissed that I'm here but enjoying the view, nonetheless.

"I'll be here, but I'm not talking," I say with my arms crossed.

The door clicks shut, and Paisley unleashes a determined glare on me.

Damn, she's beautiful. I'd do about anything to take her over that desk right now, but I know that's never happening. Which puts me in an even worse mood. Hope she's used to difficult patients.

CHAPTER 2

"Would I have what?"

Paisley

I uncross and cross my legs when Maksim Petrov walks into my office. It's a small space already, and he seems to fill it as soon as he enters, forcing me to control my breathing. Ever since New Year's Eve when his lips were on mine, I've wondered if things would have turned out differently if I hadn't found out minutes later that I was his new therapist and how much he hates my profession.

It was the fastest my libido has gone from thinking I'd chance a one-night stand with a hockey god to icing over because of what a condescending asshole he was. After that, he couldn't have gotten in my pants with a crowbar.

But that doesn't mean he doesn't affect me or that our kiss didn't either.

"We both know you're not here to partake in therapy," I say, my pen tapping on the pad of paper that rests on my lap from where I sit across from him. "Shall we play charades?"

He rests his ankle on his knee, his fingers tapping his calf. "How about you tell Gerhardt I came, participated, and then we can check that box?"

The "I came" phrasing from his lips makes me swallow

hard. But I push aside my reaction. I need to remain professional.

Mr. Gerhardt is my best friend's dad, and he's the one who threw me this bone to help elevate my business. I'm a pretty new graduate, having received my doctorate only two years ago. It's hard to start a practice. When he suggested I come counsel the Florida Fury, I jumped at the chance. But he was clear that I had to see every player.

Mr. Gerhardt also told me specifically to meet with Maksim because of his anger issues on the ice. Of course, a competitive fire is good when it comes to hockey, but sometimes Maksim takes protecting his teammates too far. He's had a lot of suspensions and fines throughout his career, which Mr. Gerhardt wants to stop. But I know if I tell Maksim that, he'll blow out of here and into Mr. Gerhardt's office to confront him, so we'll need to ease into this.

"I can't do that. Mr. Gerhardt instructed me that he wants you and the rest of the players to attend at least three sessions now. Sorry to be the bearer of bad news but those are the rules."

His mouth drops open and his forehead wrinkles. "But Drake only has to do fifteen minutes?" He sighs. "Goddamn golden boy," he murmurs under his breath.

"Well, Mr. Gerhardt did tell me Aiden got his game back recently."

He nods. "He's getting laid on the regular by a hot blonde."

"What does one have to do with the other?" I ask.

"The blonde is his lucky charm."

"Are you insinuating that sex is the reason for the improvement in his game?"

He lets out a deep, throaty laugh. "Sex does it for some guys. You've already counseled most of the team by now…

I'm sure you've heard the tales on how it works differently for everyone."

I shrug. A few have made comments to suggest as much, but the majority of the team have long-term girlfriends or wives. Some even have children. They tend to talk more about how to effectively juggle the different roles in their life. All Tweetie talked about was his girlfriend, Tedi. Or how he wants her to officially be his girlfriend but is afraid to ask. I had to bite down my smile at the big rough-and-tumble guy who's afraid to ask the girl he's been seeing to be exclusive.

"What about you? Do you think you need sex before games?" I tilt my head.

"Porn and a nap is just fine by me." He looks up from his shoe and points at me. "You're not getting me to talk."

"Knowing your preference for porn is hardly delving into your psyche," I deadpan. "You and every other man in America."

"So do you wanna know what kind of porn I prefer?" His tone is challenging.

I poise my pen over the paper. It could tell me something about him, but nothing that will reveal why he thinks he has to be the enforcer on his team. Then again, maybe I'm wrong. "If you care to share. I'm here to listen."

"Well, I like big tits and a nice ass. There has to be something to the woman."

I feel heat accosting my cheeks. I didn't think he'd actually tell me.

"How are you doing over there? Want a glass of water? An ice cube?" His mockery makes my blush disappear.

"I'm perfectly fine. Why don't you prefer to have sex before a game? Superstition?"

"Nah. Before I found out who you were, I might've enjoyed a round or two with you before a game."

I wiggle in my seat. He's getting to me, and I'm fearful I'll never make it through this appointment. "And exactly who am I?"

"A shrink. Someone who makes a living by making people believe something is wrong with them."

My pen slips from my grasp, toppling to the floor. He bends down to retrieve it and hands it back to me. When our fingers brush during the exchange, goose bumps rush up my arm.

"I don't make people believe anything is wrong with them."

"Sure, you do. Like if I told you I was into BDSM or some shit, you'd probably dive in deeper, wondering why I'd want control or to hurt someone or be hurt myself."

"I can't deny that I would want to know why you were into that."

"Maybe it's just my kink and has nothing to do with a bad upbringing, or unresolved daddy issues, or being bullied in high school." His raised eyebrow grates on my last nerve, but he's doing this so I'll kick him out of my office.

Instead, I smile sweetly, not taking the bait. "Perhaps. But it could be exactly what you just said. That's why I went to school, to figure out whether that's the case."

He stares at me a beat. A beat too long because I squirm, and he smirks, knowing the effect he has on me. "It's a shame, right?"

I clear my throat. "What is?"

"If you didn't work for the team as a therapist, I might be able to relieve that ache you're feeling between your thighs right now."

I use every muscle in my jaw to not allow it to hang open. All while my panties grow wetter. He's called me out and I hate that he's right.

"Maybe we should talk about your ego," I say.

He chuckles again. "It's very much intact."

"Exactly. Maybe there's a reason for that."

"Or maybe I'm confident in my skills. That kiss on New Year's Eve was amazing. We'd be compatible in bed."

"Sometimes you hockey players amaze me."

His mouth opens in a dazzling smile—not with perfectly straight teeth, but alluring all the same. Just like his nose that's slightly crooked, there's something so appealing about his imperfections and how they all work together to make one insanely attractive man.

"Why?" he asks.

"The confidence. Surely at some point, you were a shy kid who wasn't confident in his skills."

He laughs and his gaze dips to my legs, then he changes the subject. "Do you wear a dress every day?"

"Most." I've always been more of a dress person. Or a skirt and a blouse. Rarely do I wear pants.

"You don't have any tights on either," he says, his voice hoarse.

"Well, I'm not eight years old."

His eyes meet mine, and those sparkling blues pour heat all over my body. He's right to think we'd be compatible in bed. "Excuse me?"

"Girls wear tights. I would be wearing nylons."

His gaze returns to my legs. "Regardless, you're not wearing any."

I shake my head. "No. Now—"

"So if I was to slide my hands up your legs right now, the only barrier for my hand touching your pussy is a thin pair of panties?"

I shift in my seat again, not sure how we got this off track. "We should stick to what you're here for—therapy."

"What color are they?"

"Maksim," I plead, but my voice is breathless.

His smirk widens because he knows he's getting to me. "Would you have?"

I set the pad of paper and pen on the edge of the table by my chair. "Would I have what?"

"Slept with me? Gone home with me on New Year's Eve?"

I look around as if the answer is somewhere in this room. It's not, but I know in my bones I would have. "I don't know," I lie. "I'm not really a one-night stand kind of girl."

He nods a few times. "Who says I'm a one-night stand kind of guy?"

"You kissed me shortly after meeting me."

"You're making an assumption. Should a therapist really assume things about their client?"

I grab the pad and pen again. "Tell me then, Maksim… are you sexually promiscuous?"

He shakes his head. "I'm not looking for relations with every girl, but if it happens, it happens."

It would have been easier for me if he were a womanizing manwhore. "That's refreshing."

"Answer my question. Would you have come home with me?"

I look him directly in the eyes. "We shouldn't be talking about that. We're therapist and patient now."

"If you sign off on my slip, that part of this relationship could end."

He's so right and damn if I don't want to see his head disappear under my dress. To feel one swipe of that filthy tongue I know he has along my center. But Mr. Gerhardt trusts me, and I can't very well falsify records and still expect him to refer me out to people.

I clear my throat. It is long past time for me to get this

session back under control. "Okay, enough, Mr. Petrov." I glance at the clock and see we still have twenty minutes remaining. "Either we actually talk for the next twenty minutes, or this session doesn't count."

He relaxes back into the sofa and spreads his legs wide. "I'm Russian, only child, my parents are still married. What else do you want to know?"

"Why are you so rough on the ice?"

He shrugs a shoulder. "I'm a hockey player."

"Sure, but have you given any thought as to why you take it upon yourself to police other players for violations the refs miss, or even the ones players are already penalized for?"

He stares me dead in the eyes, his gaze intense. "I protect the ones I love."

My stomach drops and not because I didn't think that exact thing when I started watching tapes after Mr. Gerhardt told me his behavior needed correcting. My stomach drops because something rears up in me that wants him to protect me. I'd love those big arms around me, telling me everything is all right. That I won't feel this lonely all my life.

CHAPTER 3

"And you're about to lie to her."

Maksim

A few weeks have passed, and I've dodged Paisley Pearce every chance I got. Luckily, we've had some out of town games, so it was easy to make up excuses for not meeting with her.

Aiden's having a house party to celebrate Saige moving in with him—her idea, I'm sure—and Ford just texted me that he's here to pick me up.

I head down the stairs of my beachfront house to find Nadiya walking through the door with Ford right behind her. He motions like he's humping her from behind without her knowing and I roll my eyes at his immaturity.

Nadiya is a family friend from Russia, here finishing her schooling. My parents pushed me into letting her live with me because otherwise it wouldn't be safe for her to come to the States. Believe me, the girl can handle herself. I'd be scared if I pissed her off.

"Nadiya, when are you going to admit I'm the one for you and go out with me?" Ford asks, opening our fridge and grabbing a water.

"Try never." She plops her bag on the breakfast stool and grabs an apple from a bowl of fruit on the center island, sitting on a stool. "Where are you guys going?"

"Aiden's," Ford answers.

"And Saige's," I chime in. "Want to come?"

She shakes her head. "No, I'm exhausted. All I want to do is to veg out on the couch and eat greasy food."

"Cool. I'll be home later."

"I can join him, if you want a nighttime visitor," Ford says, waggling his eyebrows.

I place my hand at the back of his head, leading him to the door. Nadiya laughs because she knows Ford and his antics by now. He's not even close to her type, thank God.

We step out of my house and I push him toward his old-school Bronco. That's one thing I like about Ford, he can be down to earth on occasion. He could've hired us a ride in some fancy car, but he's chosen to drive us over.

"Stop hitting on her. You know it's never going to happen. Besides, hasn't your dick already got you in enough trouble?"

He laughs, but I hear the strain in it, and I feel like an ass for my comment. Ford climbs into his Bronco, a classic without the top. Somehow it suits Ford even though he could be driving around in a Ferrari. I think he only has the Bronco because he surfs whenever he can during the winter months.

He asks, "How do you live with her and not want to motorboat those tits?"

"I don't think of her like that."

And I don't. Nadiya isn't just a family friend. She was my best friend's little sister. That line was drawn a long time ago. When Armen died, I took on his role as her protector.

"You're lying." Ford starts the truck and pulls out of my drive, heading toward Aiden's.

Ford plays his rap music so damn loud there's no having a conversation until we're parked outside Aiden's beach house.

"You're gonna lose your damn hearing," I say while shutting off the music.

He turns off the ignition and looks at me. "You're fucking old."

I flip him off and walk up to the front door, where I ring the bell.

"Why are you ringing the bell?" Ford asks, his hand on the doorknob.

"Because this is now Saige's house and I'm sure Aiden wouldn't be cool if the two of us walked in on her naked and riding him."

The door opens.

"I'm surprised you rang the bell," Aiden says.

I point at Ford. "He wasn't going to. I had to explain that this is now Saige's house too and you wouldn't like him seeing the two of you fucking on the stairs or some shit."

Aiden leads us toward the back patio while I roll my eyes at Ford.

"We don't fuck before a party."

I know that's a bullshit lie, and we both raise our eyebrows at him.

"Just be careful in the kitchen. It's Saige's favorite," Aiden jokes, and we both groan.

"So where is the missus?" I ask, taking a beer from the tub in the back patio and sitting in a lawn chair.

"She's getting ready."

"Please tell me you didn't invite everyone from the Fury?" I ask. "Aka not Paisley the shrink." I've dodged her this long, I don't want to get cornered on what is supposed to be an enjoyable evening.

He laughs. "I'm not entirely sure who Saige invited. I doubt she would have. Although she did invite Jana, and I heard those two are tight."

Jana is Mr. Gerhardt's daughter, and ever since Aiden's game came back, he's back to being the son Mr. Gerhardt never had. He and Saige were invited over for dinner last week and if the rumor mill is right, Jana and Saige hit it off.

Ford knocks his knee against mine. "Why don't you just make up some bullshit story? Give her some 'woe is me' past that's completely made up. Let her think she's helping you, and move on?"

I still for a second. That's not a bad idea. Kind of what I was doing last time, except I used my time to hit on her with the hopes she'd grow uncomfortable and demand an end to the sessions. I'm not sure how convincing I could be if I was lying about some fake sordid past.

"She's smart. She'll probably see right through it," I admit.

"Oh please, you just lead them where they already want to go." Ford shakes his head at me. "I've been going to shrinks my entire life. Take me. Classic rich boy, so my shrink has me pegged before I even enter and thinks I have daddy issues."

"You do have daddy issues," Aiden deadpans.

Ford ignores the comment. "So I tell her a few things my dad demanded of me, even making shit up like he was my baseball coach—I mean, as if a man who runs a multi-million dollar company had time to coach his son's baseball team. Come on. Sooner or later, she's hanging on to every last piece of bullshit I'm telling her."

I don't say anything, and the doorbell ringing interrupts us.

"I'll be back," Aiden says.

The more I think about Ford's plan, the more I think it's my only hope to get out of these sessions without allowing her to try to turn me into a crying mess on her couch. I hate lying, but in certain circumstances, I have no choice. This just might be one of them.

"Tweetie!" Ford hollers as our left winger and his girl, Tedi, walk out and join us on the patio.

———

I'm at the food table when Paisley's shoulder brushes mine. I glance over and her dark curly hair blows in the wind. Her caramel-colored eyes meet mine.

"Hey, Maksim," she says.

"Paisley." I pick up some of the pig and put it on my plate.

She eyes my plate, then she's staring at the table as though she can't decide what she wants to eat. I guess there's no time like the present.

"So, I was thinking…" I start while she places some veggies on her plate.

"Is that an unusual act for you?" Before I can respond, she laughs and her hand lands on my shoulder. "I'm kidding."

The fact she couldn't keep the joke going for longer than ten seconds says she's either uncomfortable in front of me or not used to being a jokester.

"The therapy. I gave you a hard time and I've had a change of heart. I've got two more sessions and I'll happily come."

She looks around us.

"What?" I raise an eyebrow.

"I'm searching for the camera. Surely this is a joke you're playing on me."

Finally, she puts a burger on her plate. I feared she might be a vegetarian. I'm not sure I could ever date someone with that kind of self-control. Then again, I can't date Paisley for more reasons than whether or not she eats meat.

"No joke. I gave you a hard time and now…"

"The search-and-rescue mission you've had me on for the last three weeks isn't cool. Mr. Gerhardt wants feedback on who's coming to their appointments. I gave you a pass and said you stopped in last week but had an emergency and had to leave before our session commenced."

I stand still and take her in. She covered for me? Damn, that's a turn-on. "Thanks. I'll come in this week."

She nods and looks me over. "Thanks a lot, Maksim. I appreciate you changing the way this can go. I promise you, I won't bite."

"That's a shame, I like women who do." The words fall out before I can take them back.

She raises her perfectly sculpted eyebrows. For a second, I wonder if her pussy is as manicured as her eyebrows. "We really should set some ground rules."

The flush on her cheeks only spurs me to continue. I like being the reason she's blushing. "What's fun about ground rules?"

"I can't counsel you if you continue to hit on me."

I laugh and set my plate on the table, holding both hands up in the air. "Who said I was hitting on you? I'm merely vocalizing a preference."

"You need to stop flirting with me."

I slide my tongue across my bottom lip and take her in for the tenth time since she arrived. She's in a short sundress that shows off more skin than I'm comfortable with. I'm sure every man here is checking her out and wondering what she looks like with it pooled at her feet. I'm no exception. I won't deny that I want her, but I get that right now isn't the best time, what with her being my therapist. Maybe after the third visit, I can ask her out and see where this could go. Even if it's only for one night, it'd be worth it.

"Stop looking at me like that," she whispers. Her gaze darts around the immediate area as though she fears someone is watching us.

"We're both single," I say.

"I know, but we can't pursue anything. Things have to be professional."

"These limitations you're trying to put in place only make me want to push your boundaries, doctor. See how far I can get."

Her cheeks flush pink again, and I bite my lip, imagining what she looks like when she comes. "I'm serious, Maksim."

"Your tone doesn't match your words."

"Listen, I'm attracted to you, I can't deny that. But I'm your therapist now, so all of that is off the table. We have to forget the kiss."

Ah. I arch an eyebrow. "So you think about it?"

She shakes her head, picks up her plate, and stalks off.

"It's okay to admit. I beat off to the image of you in my head," I say before anyone gets closer.

Her feet stop on Aiden's deck, and I silently will her to turn around. Say she's up for breaking the rules and let's go back to her place. But instead, she shakes her head and continues walking over to the table where Jana is.

"Damn, I need to get myself under control," I say to myself.

Twenty minutes later, I approach Saige and Aiden having a couple moment. I barely see my buddy alone anymore. Saige leaves us to join the girls on the beach.

"I'm taking Ford's advice," I murmur since Aiden isn't going to like it.

He shakes his head. "You know it'll never work, right? She'll see right through you."

I shrug. "I got this. A couple sessions and she'll think I'm good. No way Gerhardt thinks I should be in therapy forever."

"Well, good luck," he says, patting me on the back. It's clear he thinks this will blow up.

We both lean on the balcony railing, looking over the beach where Paisley, Jana, Saige, and Tedi are trying to hula. Paisley's hips swing back and forth, making my dick go half chub.

"She's fucking hot, right?" I say.

"Saige? Yeah."

"Not Saige, but yeah, her too. Paisley. That long dark hair. The curls. Imagine that spread out on your pillowcase in the morning."

Aiden glances over. "And you're about to lie to her."

A sick feeling rolls through my stomach, but I pat him on the shoulder. "I'm starving. Gonna go eat."

Not wanting to dwell on this conversation, I walk away as though I didn't just eat.

Whatever. It's a means to an end. It's better this way. I've never opened up to anyone about what happened, and I don't plan on starting now.

CHAPTER 4

"Well, knowing my luck, I'll pick the bad seed and end
up watering it."

Paisley

If I thought trying to push down my attraction to Maksim was hard when he was in front of me, it actually feels even harder sitting in the Gerhardt's suite in the arena and watching him perform on the ice. How can someone so big and powerful appear so graceful while skating? He's like a gliding freight train.

I nibble on the cheese and meat I took off the charcuterie board. The food's amazing up here, but I wouldn't mind some nachos or a big pretzel. Isn't that half the fun of attending sports games? I've been coming to Fury games since Mr. Gerhardt bought the team. Jana and I were given the okay to roam the arena during games. We'd find open seats in the nosebleeds, Jana always interested in which boys we'd meet, but my eyes would linger on the game.

There's always been something about a hockey player I can't ignore. I've had crushes on so many of the players that I've been privileged to meet during parties and dinners at the Gerhardts' over the years that I've lost count.

Being like their adopted daughter entitled me to see the behind-the-scenes of the life the players live. Sure, some are on the straight and narrow, but I've accidentally walked in on my fair share of players in bathrooms and bedrooms with women who aren't their wives. Others are pure egotistical assholes when you meet them in person. It all served to take the shine off them, but it didn't keep me from being drawn to them.

Counseling the Fury team these past months has only been hard with Maksim. With the rest of the players, I'm able to remain professional, and I really feel as though I'm making a difference. But with Maksim, the way his eyes smolder when he looks at me and the intensity in his baby blues… I find my body drawn his way. Our next appointment is in two days and it's occupied my mind since Saturday at Aiden and Saige's party.

"Who is it this year?" Jana sits down next to me, stealing an olive from the board. She pops it in her mouth.

I couldn't be more opposite than Jana. I've felt like the fugly one all of our lives. She's got the blonde hair, the blue eyes, the perfect cheekbones, and flawless skin. I, on the other hand, have unruly curly brown hair, brown eyes, and there's nothing sculpted on my body. My curves are more rolling hillsides to her sleek lines.

"What are you talking about?" I look at her.

She looks around behind us to make sure no one is paying us any attention and leans in. "Maksim Petrov?" Her smile says she already knows she's right. "I saw you two at the party last weekend. I haven't seen you blush that much since we were sixteen and Troy Iverness came to dinner at my house." She laughs. "He thought there was something medically wrong with you because you kept staring at him and not saying a word."

"Funny, Jana," I say, remembering that moment.

She grabs another green olive. "Seriously though, he's hot and he's got all that anger out on the ice. I bet you could help him work some of it off in the bedroom." Her eyebrows waggle.

"You know I don't sleep with hockey players," I say.

Sadly, it's true. Regardless of the way they've always appealed to me, I've seen the other side and it's not pretty. Take Troy Iverness, for example. I thought he was the best father and husband when he'd come over to the Gerhardts', only to find out he was sleeping with the nanny. Talk about idols being knocked from pedestals.

"That's ridiculous. Everyone knows there are bad seeds in every bunch."

"Well, knowing my luck, I'll pick the bad seed and end up watering it."

She laughs. "You're so hard on yourself."

I shrug. "You'd be too."

I was the poorest in my private school in high school. Only got to go because when my parents divorced, my mom made my dad pay for it. He could barely afford it while trying to support his new family. Then I got wait-listed while all my friends got into their colleges of choice because their parents either knew someone or were alums themselves. Mr. Gerhardt pulled the final string for me that got me into Vanderbilt. I'm still paying off those loans.

Jana graduated from Vanderbilt too, and while I went on to get my doctorate, she came home and has been at her dad's side in his business. One day this team will probably be hers.

"Plus, I'm the team's therapist now. I can't sleep with him now anyway."

She rests her chin in her palm, her perfectly manicured nails tapping her cheek. "Still, you gotta wonder with a man like him. Where does all that pent-up energy go? I think for sure the bedroom."

Jealousy picks at me while I watch Jana's mind shift to what it would be like to sleep with Maksim. She shrugs then drinks from her martini and plops another two olives in her glass. The girl loves olives to the point of grossness.

"Petrov is sent to the sin bin again," the announcer calls on the televisions that line the walls of the suite.

My gaze falls to the Jumbotron, where they show a replay of Maksim grabbing the jersey of another player and punching him.

"Goddamn it," Mr. Gerhardt murmurs behind me. "Jana, may I have a word with Paisley?"

Jana cringes and stands. "Sure, Dad, but don't take it out on Paisley."

He winds his hand around her waist and kisses her cheek. "I know. Go find your mother." Mr. Gerhardt takes his daughter's seat and stares at the big screen above the ice. "How are things going with Maksim?"

I busy myself with piling cheese on a cracker. "It's good. We've had one session so far."

"Good. He's not giving you a hard time, is he?" He twirls his scotch around his cup and brings the glass to his lips. "He can be difficult. Didn't seem happy when I told him about counseling."

I smack on a fake smile. "It's early days and you know I can't discuss with you—"

He raises his hand. "Understandable." He nods a few times.

I think I've appeased him until the crowd laughs and our eyes fly to the screen again. Maksim is spraying water from his bottle onto a fan of the opposing team on the other side of the plexiglass.

"This is the kind of shit he needs to stop. Next thing I know he's going to start a bench brawl." He turns my way. "Maksim is a great guy. When I recruited him, he and his family were so thankful, and don't get me wrong, he gets results on the ice, but that temper…" He shakes his head. "Well, I hope for his sake you fix him."

He pats me on the hand and walks away.

Fix.

I hate that word. As if something is wrong with someone and they're seeing me because they need rewiring. I'm not a car mechanic and their engine isn't broken. Whatever the reason for Maksim's blowups, I know it will be hard to get him to let me in. The odd thing is, it's only on the ice. Off the ice, Maksim is known for making the rounds at children's hospitals and autographing anything a fan gives him. It's like a switch goes off in him once his skates hit the ice.

———

The game ends and I'm stuffing my phone in my purse when Jana swings her arm through mine.

"Dad's got a request."

I groan because I'd bet a month's rent of my dinky apartment that the request isn't something I'll be thrilled about. "What?"

"He wants us to head over to Carmelo's."

My forehead crinkles. "The Fury bar? Why?"

"He wants us to make sure they're behaving." She shrugs.

"Since when are we chaperones for the team?"

She laughs. "Come on. It'll be fun. We need a night together that doesn't involve binging Netflix and eating junk food."

Jana's right, but I'm not telling her that. Lately, when she's not out on a date, she joins me in a Netflix and chill session that I'm sure is the antithesis of what that phrase is supposed to mean. I stopped going to bars because when I go with Jana, I usually end up playing wingwoman and entertaining whatever guy the guy who's interested in her calls over. For some reason, that guy is always the shyest guy ever and getting him to speak is like trying to pry open up a vault with a crowbar—an exercise in futility.

"Okay, then I guess that's what we're doing." I don't bother putting up a fight because I've had a few drinks and the idea of being around Maksim is appealing. Maybe seeing him in his element will help me figure out some things about him.

Twenty minutes later, we arrive at Carmelo's and are seated in a booth in the bar area.

I pick up a menu. "I think I'm going to eat."

Jana snatches it from my grasp. "What are you going to do? Eat a rack of ribs or a big bowl of spaghetti right as the team gets here?"

I grab the menu back. "First off, I'm a grown adult and if I want to eat, I eat. Second of all, what does it matter? I'm their therapist, not their eye candy."

She grips the edge of the menu and I pull it back. Soon we're having a tug-of-war with it.

"Maksim will be here," she stage-whispers.

"So?"

"So I know you like him, and having spaghetti all over your face isn't going to make him crazy with lust." I release the menu and she flies back into the booth with an oomph. "Seriously?"

"You're playing games." I point at her. "Did your dad even really want us to come here?"

She grins.

"Jana!"

"What? I saw you at the party. You like him."

I shake my head. "What's not to like? But I'm his therapist now, so that ship is lost somewhere in the Bermuda Triangle."

Her shoulders fall. "Come on. Put yourself out there. I think you'll reap the benefits. I see the way he watches you."

I sigh. She means well. "I know you live a privileged life and all, but you're aware that if I sleep with Maksim Petrov—or any other Fury player—that I could be arrested, right? It's illegal."

She waves me off, which I expected. "That's not going to happen."

"Maybe not, but I could also lose my license to practice, my livelihood."

She shakes her head. "Not if he's in agreement."

"Jana—it can't happen."

I love my best friend with all my heart, but she's never had a consequence to an action in her life. Sure, her dad can be hard on her sometimes and expects a lot out of her, but at the end of the day, she knows he has her back. He can buy or influence his way out of anything bad happening to his only child.

The waitress comes over and I snatch the menu back from Jana and open it.

"We'll have two dry martinis with double olives," Jana orders.

I point at her. "That's for her. I'll have a glass of chianti and the rigatoni with cream sauce."

Jana rolls her eyes and huffs. She can continue doing that while she watches me eat.

"Bread?" the waitress asks.

"Yes," I answer at the same time Jana says, "No."

I nod. "Please."

Jana shakes her head. "What am I going to do with you?"

"The same thing you've done with me our whole lives… pester me until I call mercy."

We both laugh. That's why I love our friendship. We couldn't be more different, but we've clicked ever since freshmen year of high school when I was on my period and leaked onto my skirt and Jana was the only one with the guts to tell me.

My laughter dies when the door of Carmelo's opens and small groups of large men trickle in. A lot of them say hello to us, then head over to their favorite booths.

I don't know what Jana was worried about. They don't want anything to do with us. She's the owner's daughter after all. No one hangs with the boss's daughter.

That is, until a large body slides into my booth without an invitation. I look over to find a pair of crystal-blue eyes rimmed with black lashes staring at me. "What's up, doc?"

A vision of him naked on a stretcher and me with my stethoscope out, listening for his heartbeat while he opens up my white doctor's jacket flashes in my mind.

Get it together, Paisley. He doesn't affect you. Make him realize that fact right now.

I straighten my shoulders and open my mouth, but of course nothing comes out.

CHAPTER 5

Maksim

I blink to make sure that that's actually Paisley in the booth, that I didn't conjure her up in my mind. After a shitty game where I spent more time in the sin box than on the ice, I need a few shots and a good meal.

Ford heads toward the other guys while I beeline to the other side of Carmelo's and slide in next to Paisley. "What's up, doc?"

Her eyebrows raise and I chuckle. It's a well-known fact the Fury hang here after every home game, so she can't be surprised to see me. Some of us only stay for a meal and others will be here until closing.

Rachel, the usual waitress, comes over and places a glass of red wine in front of Paisley and a martini that holds more olives than vodka in front of Jana. "Usual, Maks?" Her hand rests on my shoulder.

"That'd be great. Thanks."

She smiles and walks away.

Paisley's having some kind of nonverbal conversation with Jana, but when Jana spots me watching, she smiles and sets her attention on me. "Nice game, Maksim."

"We both know it was a crap game and your dad's gonna have my ass for it."

She waves me off. "No. He loves you. Thinks of all you guys as his sons." She fishes an olive from the glass and slides it off the toothpick.

"You seemed more angry than usual," Paisley says. I'm surprised to hear her chime in.

"I thought you didn't watch hockey," I say, remembering her telling me that on New Year's Eve.

She shrugs. "Jana drags me to some games."

"What?" Jana's forehead wrinkles. "Ouch." She leans down and rubs her leg, giving her best friend an evil stare.

I don't call them out on their bullshit. I'm confident I'll get it out of Paisley in due time.

Rachel brings me my vodka straight up. "Hungry tonight?"

I glance at the two women seated at the table. "Are you guys eating?"

"No," Jana says at the same time Paisley says, "Yes."

Again, they have some conversation with their eyes. Watching their friendship play out reminds me of Armen and me. We were like brothers.

"What are you having?" I ask Paisley.

"Pasta."

I look at Rachel. "I'll have the mussels dish I usually get."

"Coming right up."

I stretch my arm across the top of the booth and Paisley watches the move intently. "So, what brings you ladies here? Don't be shy, you can say it's me."

Jana laughs and shakes her head. "Hockey players and their egos."

"We came here as babysitters because Ford can't seem to stay out of the press."

Paisley speaks the truth. Ford's been a little out of control, but now that he's gonna be a daddy in a few months, I'm sure he'll calm down. Or knowing him, he might try to get it all out of his system.

"Maybe I need a babysitter," I say and wink at Paisley.

She sips her wine, ignoring my flirtation.

"You need one on the ice," Jana says. "Why are you so angry out there?"

I look at my boss's daughter, hoping what I'm about to say will get back to my boss so he will get off my ass. "I'm not angry. I'm protecting my boys. Someone has to do it when the ref has a blind eye."

She nods. "That's kind of noble, but don't you care about your own game?"

"That is my game. I'm a defender. I defend."

"Some would say that you're taking the rules into your own hands," Jana argues, poking another olive with her toothpick and bringing it to her lips. Jana's not my type, but if she were and she wasn't the boss's daughter, I'd find her eating an olive highly erotic.

Maybe I can convince Paisley to have one.

"Maybe." I shrug. "Some might say that, but I make sure my boys skate off that ice at the end of every game."

Paisley takes another sip of her wine, pretending she isn't listening to our conversation.

"You're an interesting person, Maksim." Jana smiles, so I'll take it as a compliment. "I'm heading to the jukebox before Ford takes all the songs." She slides out of the booth.

"Guess that only leaves us." I grin at Paisley.

She sets her glass down and her fingers twirl the stem in a circle. "Feel free to join your teammates."

I glance over my shoulder where some are already hanging with the groupies while others are shooting the shit with one another. "I'd hate to leave you alone."

"I don't need a babysitter."

"According to you, I do though." I smile brightly and get rewarded with a small chuckle that she stops abruptly.

"Actually, I said Ford."

"Looks like Jana's got that under control." I nod across the room to where Jana is lecturing Ford about something over by the jukebox.

Rumors have spread that Jana might end up taking over the team soon because Gerhardt wants to bring another professional sports team into our town. The change would be interesting, that's for sure.

"She's tough," Paisley says.

"How long have you guys been friends?" I ask before taking a sip of my drink.

"You do know there's an empty side of the booth over there." She points at the other side.

I chuckle. "I'm fine where I am, but thanks for your concern."

Rachel brings our dishes at the same time, placing them in front of us.

"Looks great. Thanks, Rach." I slide over to the other side of the booth, and Paisley looks at me as though she's trying to figure out what I'm up to. I answer her unasked question. "I like you, and if you're a loud chewer, I don't want that to ruin this budding relationship."

She stares blankly at me.

"Come on. Haven't you ever been interested in someone just to find out they have some trait that drives you crazy?"

She unwraps her silverware and places the napkin in her lap. "Can't say I have."

"Well, think of it this way, I like you too much to find out if you have one just yet." I wink, and she shakes her head and forks her pasta. "I will say one thing though, I love that you ordered food."

"Do most people you're interested in not eat?"

I laugh, but more times than not, they don't. Or they eat something super small, like a side salad, definitely not a plate of pasta. "They do, but it's different."

She sets down her fork, wipes her mouth. "I'm curious, how many girls are we talking about?"

"Do you really want to compare numbers right now?" I arch an eyebrow.

She shrugs. "I don't care anyway."

"Doesn't matter, I guess. Even if you say one person, that'll be too high for me. I hate the idea of you with another man."

Her fork slips from her fingers this time, resting on her plate of pasta. "What are you doing?"

Is my game that off?

"I thought my intentions were clear. I'm hitting on you."

"I'm your therapist. You can't hit on me." Then she mumbles something, but all I make out is the word Jana.

"Okay then, let's just enjoy a dinner together." Maybe that will help her relax.

She forks her pasta once again and continues eating, never looking at me. We eat in silence for a while.

I glance around the room to see where Jana disappeared to, but I find her with Aiden and Saige, all of their eyes on Paisley and me. "Don't look now, but we're being watched."

Paisley shakes her head. "I never should've come here."

"Why do you say that?" I down a mussel and pick up my fork.

"Because people are now speculating about the two of us and I have to remain professional. Having people think I'm your postgame piece of ass isn't going to earn me the respect I need in order to do my job."

The bite in her tone makes me smile. I like this feisty side of her. Still, I never thought about how it would look to the other guys. I'm not known for sleeping with puck bunnies, but if they start speculating that I'm nailing the therapist... she's right, they might not take her seriously. And because I have too much respect for her, I decide to cool it with my flirting.

"I'm sorry. You're right. How about we just eat our meals?"

Her fork hovers over her plate of pasta and she gives me an appreciative smile. "Thank you."

A few beats of silence pass, and I hear Ford's voice carrying over everyone else's in this place.

"So... I might actually be a big fan of hockey," she says.

My fist pounds on the table. "I knew it." Then my gaze scatters across the room. The music is too loud for anyone to hear me. "Favorite position?"

"Goalie."

I snap my fingers. "Damn. Should I call over Roadie?"

She shakes her head. "No. Plus he's married with two kids."

Although that doesn't stop some players, I don't say that. "True, but I'm sure he'd sign your tits."

"Maybe my ass too?" She feigns excitement.

I laugh because we both know she's not that kind of woman. "What is it about hockey? What spurred your interest?"

"Mr. Gerhardt buying the team. I didn't know anything about the sport until he brought the Fury down here. Jana always dragged me along to the games because she didn't want to go alone. I fell in love with it."

"I've loved it since I was old enough to skate. Probably before that. My dad played on a men's team when I was younger, and my mom would take me all the time. Funny enough, that's how I met my best bud, Armen." The words are out of my mouth before I can stop them.

Her eyes widen and I love the genuine interest in them. "Does Armen play?"

"No," I answer truthfully without giving her any other information. She's my therapist, and if I go into Armen's story, I might as well open a vein and bleed out my pent-up emotions all over her.

"I guess I assumed you both played professionally for some reason."

"Nope." I shake my head and press my lips together. "You and I meet again in two days."

She nods.

"I heard someone say you're traveling with us?" I ask, hoping it's true. I might have to cool it in front of my teammates, but who cares what happens behind closed doors.

Her face scrunches up. "No, I don't think so."

"That's what I heard."

She must hear the conviction in my voice because she puts down her fork and pulls out her phone, scrolling through. Her jaw falls open and she looks at me. "You're right. Mr. Gerhardt just sent me an email." She shakes her head. "Good thing I don't have too many clients to maneuver around."

"Just wait. Do you know how to play Oh Hell?"

She shakes her head.

"I'll teach you."

Her eyebrows shoot up.

I place my hands in the air. "Platonic. I swear."

Maybe I need to take what I can get for the time being, but I'm not giving up.

CHAPTER 6

"Maybe I should come back."

Paisley

When I was younger, I occasionally traveled with the Gerhardts on the Fury's road games, but we'd take their private jet. I often daydreamed about what it would be like to sit on the plane with the players. What did they do on the plane? Was it like any other plane ride and everyone kept to themselves? As I got older, I wondered if they had strippers and alcohol over-filling their glasses, a constant party.

I never would've thought that half of them play video games, four of them play cards, and the rest of them read or mess around on their phones.

"Fucking hell!" Ford screams, slamming his cards on the table.

I pretend to be reading a book. Maksim asked if I wanted to play, said he'd teach me, but I politely declined. Maksim and Aiden high-five and Ford shakes his head, sulking in his seat.

"You're the worst loser ever," Maksim says.

"I swear you guys fixed the game."

From what I know about Ford—other than the fact that he just got some random girl pregnant, because that's all over the media—his family is rich. *Über*rich. I'm fairly sure he has a trust fund, but rumors are that he can't touch it until he's done with hockey. Because Ford managed to get Mr. Gerhardt to excuse him from meeting with me, the only other thing I know about him is that he's a crazy skilled skater and makes killer hard passes through the neutral zone, feeding Aiden the puck. Which says to me he's not all about being the center of attention like people assume. Not that he does much to dissuade people from having that opinion of him.

Aiden and Maksim look at one another and crack up laughing. "Who, us?"

I bite down my smile and bury my head in my book. The last thing I need is to get pulled into their conversation. I've reread the same sentence five times already. A big body takes the seat next to mine. I glance over, expecting Maksim.

"Mind if I sit here?" Ford asks, signaling for the flight attendant to bring him a drink.

I shake my head and continue reading.

"Why do chicks always read on planes?" he asks.

"What the fuck are you doing, Ford?" Maksim says from across the way.

"Just talking to our good therapist here." Ford smiles at me.

His dark golden hair gives him a beach vibe, but Ford's smile and charisma are all privilege. As if he was born knowing how to get his way, how to get people to bend rules. I'd bet that over the years, he's perfected that craft, assuming nothing will come hard in his life now.

"You got out of therapy, remember?" Maksim says.

I don't dare look up because jealousy is clear in his tone.

Ford puts up his hand. "This is an A and B conversation. C yourself out." Then he situates himself so he's facing me. "What are you reading?"

"A nonfiction book." I show him the cover of the book that a college friend wrote about her own journey through therapy.

"I thought it'd be some racy romance."

"Do you read?" I tilt my head, keeping my finger as a placeholder in my book.

"I don't know how." His lips tip down and he gives me the biggest puppy dog eyes.

"Bullshit."

He chuckles. "Why do you say that? Maybe I'm one of those athletes who got out of earning my grades because I was needed on the team."

"I know of your family, Ford. I'm pretty sure it was demanded that you get a great education from top-notch schools."

The flight attendant interrupts, bringing over a sparkling clear drink with a wedge of lemon and setting it in front of Ford.

"What are you drinking?" I ask.

"Sparkling water with a lemon. We have a game tonight." He sips it and sets it on the table in front of us. "Let's talk some more about what you know about me."

"Yeah, men like you do like to talk about themselves."

He stares at me for a beat, then a wicked smile forms. "You think you have me all figured out, don't you?"

I shake my head. "I don't know anything about you. Not anything other than what the media says, which is probably only fifty percent accurate."

"Well, I am having a baby with a one-night stand." He confirms the rumors surrounding his name at the moment.

"And how do you feel about that?"

It's a question I ask all the time in my practice, and I usually wouldn't pry as much during a regular conversation like the one we're having, but my gut is telling me that Ford wants to talk to someone about what's going on. Maybe that's why he's sitting next to me. Why he would pick me, I have no idea. The man can afford far more brilliant minds to guide him through this change in his life.

He shrugs. "Terrified. I'm not sure where I fit in. My dad's pissed. I kind of like that he's so mad, but now he wants me to be part of the family business even more."

I nod and glance around, finding Maksim watching us intently. "Why is your dad mad?" I ask in a low voice.

He scoffs. "Because how cliche can I be? Not being careful and getting a girl I don't know pregnant. Regardless, the baby is a Jacobs and that comes with a lot of responsibility. He worries about Britney not being able to deal with the spotlight. Or that's what he says, but what he really means is she doesn't fit the mold."

He sips his drink again and I put the bookmark in my book and tuck it at my side. "Britney is the baby's mother?"

He nods. "I met her after a game in New York."

"The baby is innocent in this situation," I say, offering advice not as a therapist but as a woman.

He nods again. "I know, but how do I parent a child when I've got my own issues with my father I've never been able to figure out? I don't want to be like him with my child, but at the same time, that's all I know."

I suck in my lips to stop myself from smiling. Ford Jacobs is worried about what kind of father he'll be, that he could end up being a replica of his own father and that terrifies him. There's more to this man than you see at first glance.

My hand lands on his forearm and he looks at me. It's not hard to see why women find him so attractive. He's got that Ralph Lauren model thing going for him. As though he belongs in khakis on a mega yacht. But mixed with that are layers that makes a woman want to peel them away. Not this woman, but I have no doubt many have tried.

"The decision of what kind of father you want to be to your child is completely up to you. There's no gene that determines that, Ford. If you don't want to be with your child the way your father was with you, then don't be. It's that simple and that hard. It's not uncommon for new parents to struggle with their new roles, but you can do this. You just have to decide to do it and then put the work in to make it happen."

A long, deep breath leaves his mouth and his eyes turn soft. "Thank you. Now can you help me beat the shit out of them at Oh Hell?"

I laugh and he laughs harder. A big shadow appears over us, and we both look up to see Maksim standing in the aisle of the plane.

Ford grabs his drink and stands, patting his friend on the shoulder. "Relax, big guy, just talking." Ford winks at me and takes the magazine out of Aiden's hands, to which Aiden mutters his displeasure.

Maksim sits down next to me without asking. "Aiden usually likes to explore the cities we travel to, so why don't you come to my room for our therapy session?" His voice is low, so no one else hears him.

"Okay." That will be our second session, which means we'll be done with the therapy requirements put forth by Mr. Gerhardt after one more.

"Cool. See you then."

Just when I think he'll stay seated next to me and try to

flirt and make me blush like always, he walks back to his seat. I guess he did take it to heart when I told him at Carmelo's that I need to remain professional. Although it warms my heart that he heard me, my body yearns for the man who didn't accept the barriers I erected. Where did that guy go?

---

*A*fter the plane lands, we go to the hotel, check in, and thankfully I don't have to stay on the same floor as the players.

I take the elevator down to the players' floor and find security standing guard at the end of the hall. He nods to me, and I walk down the long hallway to the room Maksim texted me earlier.

With my laptop bag at my side and my hair still up in a semi-messy bun after the flight, I look professional, so there's no reason anyone should think anything is going on except me counseling one of the players. Still, I'd rather none of them caught me outside Maksim's door. I knock and no one answers, so I knock again.

Aiden answers the door with the phone at his ear. "I told you to come."

He signals with his hand to come in, and I step into the room. There are two queen beds, an open suitcase on the chair in the corner, and the suit jacket Maksim was wearing has been thrown on the bed, his shoes at the foot of the bed.

"Paisley just got here. I'll FaceTime you. Love you." Aiden hangs up the phone. "Saige says hello."

I smile. "Tell her hello next time you speak to her."

He laughs. "That will be in literally five minutes. She

used to travel with me, but she had to stay back this time. She's not happy about it." He sits on the edge of the bed and puts on his sneakers. "I think she might actually be a little worried." His smile says he kind of likes the idea of her being jealous. "Hopefully she'll get used to being with a professional hockey player and not worry all the time."

"I'm sure she will." I look around, unsure where to sit.

Aiden laughs. "Maybe you can teach him how to be less of a slob." He picks up the giant suitcase and dumps it on the floor, waving his hand for me to take a seat. "He'll be out in a second."

As he says it, the bathroom door opens. With steam billowing out, Maksim steps out in only a towel as though it's happening in a dream. A very erotic dream.

"See you two later."

I blink to get out of my daydream.

Aiden is talking to Maksim, then he turns to me. "See you, Paisley."

I wave, my vocal cords unable to function. Maksim Petrov is built as though he was carved from granite. My body sighs at the thought of him hovering over me and my fingers itch to know how the ripples of his stomach feel.

"Sorry, but I hate airplanes and I felt like I needed to shower for you."

"Maybe I should come back." I stand to leave. This is hardly professional.

"Don't be silly. I meant to grab my clothes before, I just forgot them." He comes closer to me.

My breath hitches in my throat when I see droplets of water trickle down his body. My mouth waters, begging me to stick out my tongue and swipe off a few. Just as I think he's going to corner me in the chair, he bends down, keeping his hand secure on where the sides of the towel come together. He picks up some clothes, then I see his ass in the towel while he walks back to the bathroom.

"I'll just be a second." The bathroom door shuts.

My body slides down the chair from all my muscles turning to mush. How will I ever keep this guy in the client category when I'm on the cusp of begging him to make me come every time he's around? I'm in deeper than I think.

CHAPTER 7

"Don't go."

Maksim

smile at my reflection in the mirror, dressing in a T-shirt and shorts. She wants me. I saw her dilated eyes and open mouth. But I have to take this slow because she's not going to just jump my bones. Something tells me Paisley has the willpower of a saint.

Walking out of the bathroom, I compose myself and sit on the bed, leaning my back against the headboard and stretching my legs out in front of me. She crosses her legs and pulls out a pad of paper.

"Ready to get started?" she asks, her thumbs pressing on the screen of her phone.

"Do you need a drink? You sound parched." How I'm saying this with a straight face, I have no fucking clue because the pink flush to her cheeks makes me want to lean over that chair and kiss the living shit out of her. Take out that messy bun and see those gorgeous curls fan over her shoulders. I cross my legs, adjusting my half chub.

"No. Thank you." Her voice cracks, but I don't offer again. I need to play this casual.

"What do you want to know?"

She skeptically glances at me. "Why are you so eager to get started?"

"Because the faster we get through three of these, the faster you'll be in my bed."

She inhales a deep breath. "Maksim."

"Yeah?"

Just when I think she's going to give me a talking-to, she taps her pen. "What was your childhood like?"

I guess this is therapy. "It was like any other normal life."

"What about familial pressure? Did you ever feel like you had no option but to play hockey?"

I lick my bottom lip, trying my damnedest to concentrate. "Only pressure I felt was from myself. Sure, my parents wanted me to play, but…" I don't finish. For some reason, I forgot the bullshit story I was going to tell her.

She jots a few things on the paper. "And no siblings. What's that like?"

"Do you have any siblings?" I ask.

"We're not talking about me. Answer the question."

"I like this stern side of you. Turns me on." I pat the bed next to me.

She acts as though she didn't see me. "Let's stay on task."

"I liked not having any siblings. I had good friends." Which is true. Armen was my best friend and a brother to me.

"How is your parents' marriage?"

I don't much care for these questions. "What about your parents?"

She places the pad of paper in her lap, the pen following. "I'm not sure this is going to work."

"What?"

She waves her finger between us. "You can't keep flirting with me."

She uncrosses her legs and plants both feet on the floor. Fear courses through me that she's going to leave the room.

"I'm trying not to, but I want you."

She closes her eyes and inhales. "We've been over this."

I slide down to the corner of the bed, breaking the distance between us. "Tell me you don't feel this."

She shakes her head. "It's just attraction. Nothing more. We can do these sessions, I'll sign off, and you can move on."

"And then you'll allow me to take you out on a date?" I reach forward, but she squeezes her pad of paper with both hands, making me retract mine.

"No. I still work for the Fury." She shakes her head and packs up her bag. "We can be friends and that's all."

I watch her put the pad of paper in the bag, along with the pen. When she stands, I do too, cornering her. "You'll never quench the thirst you have for me with someone else. I know I never will."

She looks up at me, and her caramel eyes blind me to any reason why we can't be together. I step closer.

"What do you need from me in order to cross the line?" I ask in a low, rough voice.

She shakes her head vehemently. "Nothing. I can't. There are ethics involved."

"Who the fuck cares? Do you think I'd tell anyone? We're both adults."

"People will find out. Plus, I know right now it looks all great, but if this goes sour, you could sue me. I could lose everything."

I lean forward, reaching around her, and grab the small notepad that comes with the room, along with the pen. I scribble a note and sign my name then date it before handing it to her. "This should handle it."

She reads over where I wrote. "I am willingly sleeping

with Paisley Pearce and firing her from being my therapist regardless of what Mr. Gerhardt wants. He doesn't own me."

Her expression falters and she shoots me that look. The one that makes me see her as an innocent injured bird who needs to be loved and cared for. Damn if I don't want to be her reason to wake up in the morning. "You're going to do this just so you can sleep with me?"

I shake my head. "This isn't just about sex. I want to explore this."

"And Mr. Gerhardt and your therapy?"

"I can deal with him and his demands that I have therapy at another time. For now, we'll keep this quiet."

She steps back but hits the edge of the desk. I lean over and place my hands on the desk on either side of her hips, caging her in.

"So you get exactly what you want—no therapy and to sleep with me."

"I told you, I don't need therapy." I take the tie thing from her hair, watching the long dark curls fall down over her shoulders and back. "Tell me you don't want me, and I'll back off."

Our eyes lock. She's searching for something, but I don't know what. "I can't say that."

I feel almost buoyant. "Let me kiss you." My voice is soft and cajoling.

Her breath labors and staggers, so I place my hand over her heart, dangerously close to her breast. Picking up her other hand, I place it on my chest. "See? I'm just as nervous."

"No one will know?" Her gaze darts to my lips.

I shake my head, narrowing the distance between us. "Not a soul."

"Okay," she agrees.

I'm so fucking happy that I freeze for a moment before I bend down, bringing my lips within inches of hers. I smile and my tongue slides out, skating over my bottom lip. I'm ready to kiss the shit out of this woman—finally. I'm half a second away from what I've wanted for months when the hotel room door flies open.

"Saige, you're being unreasonable," Aiden's voice sounds.

Paisley slides out from between my arms, rushing to collect her stuff.

"Don't go," I whisper.

I look down at my tented shorts. Fuck. I quickly turn and tuck my hard-on under the elastic waistband of my track shorts, covering it with my T-shirt before facing him again.

"Sorry, guys, I'll be out in a second. I forgot this." Aiden holds up a picture of Saige on a wooden stick.

"Oh no, I was just leaving." Paisley looks at the corny picture. "Cute idea."

"Paisley…" I say.

"Good luck tonight, guys." She never looks at me, and she's out the door before I can protest further.

"You fucking idiot," I say to Aiden who's still talking to Saige, oblivious to what he just interrupted.

Then he leaves the room and I flop forward on the mattress and scream into my pillow. After a moment, I slide up against the headboard, turning on the television. I guess it's porn and a nap. At least I don't have to worry about a change of routine fucking up my game.

*M*id-game, I catch sight of Paisley sitting in the front row. Usually she's up in the suites, but Mr. Gerhardt didn't come with us this trip. She's eating a pretzel and watching the game, but every time I get close to the glass, her gaze diverts away from me. I had her right there, then fucking Aiden had to fuck it up for me.

Sometime in the second period, McGregor high sticks Aiden and red veils my eyes. It's a cheap shot against one of our best players, so screw McGregor. I skate over and push him into the boards. He falls and loses his stick. Glancing back at me, he has that look in his eyes, the challenge telling me he thinks he can kick my ass. Let's see about that.

I throw down my gloves, but before we get into it, I hear the buzzer. Satisfaction that my team just scored fills me, which only pisses off McGregor more.

The referees skate next to us, ready to get between us if it gets too dirty. This is when I wonder what it was like to play hockey back in the day. Players like Bobby Orr or Paul Coffey, when it wasn't all talk about concussions and political shit. You went out on the ice and you played hard as fuck to win that game no matter what it took.

I grab McGregor's jersey and use it to flail him around a bit. He throws the first punch, nailing me in the eye, but I hammer back another one. Soon both our fists are flying, and we each have a hand on a jersey. But way too soon, the refs break it up and we're thrown in the penalty box.

As I sit there, my gaze lingers on Paisley. She's biting her lip and staring at me, her look soft yet concerned. Heckles and chirping come from the opposing fans surrounding me in the penalty box. Toronto fans are faithful ones, and they're pissed I went after one of their guys.

Midway through my penalty, I can't take it anymore and raise both my hands, flipping off the fans. Of course, boos ring out. Because it would be no other way, the cameras catch it and there I am on the Jumbotron. Either I own it or show I'm soft, so I own it, standing and flipping off the entire arena.

When I'm finally out of the box, I rush back out on the ice and do my fucking job. The one I was hired to do. The one that pays me a shitload of money. I couldn't care less if the Toronto fans hate me. It's all part of the game. I have to be intimidating and show no weakness if I want people to fear me and fear fucking with the rest of my boys on the ice.

My repercussion comes after a two-to-one win. Coach calls me into the office and asks me to shut the door.

"Flipping off the entire arena? A bit much, no?" He sits down and pours himself a glass of Jack Daniels.

"You should have heard what they said."

"They're fans, they're supposed to razz you. You're the professional athlete, being paid millions. You need to control yourself." He sips his drink.

I debate asking for one. I could use a shot to calm me down. All I want to do is fuck Paisley Pearce until I pass out, but I've ruined my chance by not being able to hold it all together for three therapy sessions. That pissed me off, and I took it out on McGregor.

"I'm sorry, Coach, it won't happen again."

He downs the rest of his drink. "I hate to break it to you, but people don't like enforcers as much anymore. We both know there's a place for them and we need guys like you to keep the other team honest and not go after our high scorers, but you have to do better with the fans." He pours himself another drink.

"Got it."

"I hope so. Now go play whatever video game is cool right now, or go get laid, go hunting and kill some wild animal—whatever you need to do to get some of this temper out of you." He shoos me away with his hand and I leave his office.

I'm not going to do any of those things, but I am going to deal with Paisley. That somehow feels equally as dangerous as dealing with a wild animal.

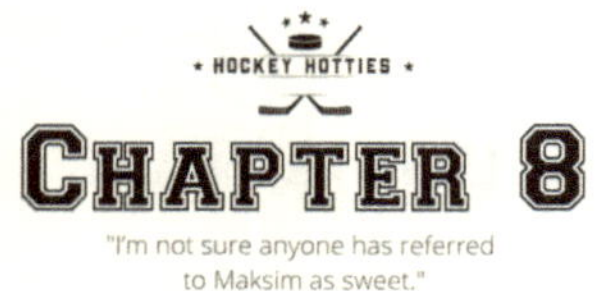

CHAPTER 8

"I'm not sure anyone has referred
to Maksim as sweet."

Paisley

"I can't control the man, Mr. Gerhardt." I pace my hotel room floor, the television paused on the *Sex and the City* rerun I was watching.

"He's not getting any better. Pretty soon he's going to get himself in more trouble than he's worth."

I blow out a breath.

"I mean, Canada is known for their polite people," he says. "The fans couldn't have said anything that bad."

"I'm not sure why he did it. He's not exactly the easiest man to crack," I say, regretting my words immediately.

"I get the whole Russian silence act, but something tells me you have it in you to get to the bottom of this issue. Protecting your teammates is one thing. Spraying fans with water bottles and flipping them off is another. Fans are the ones who pay his salary."

"I'll see what I can do," I say.

A knock on the door sounds. For a moment, I'd forgotten I ordered room service. I tuck the phone between my ear and my shoulder, opening the door and expecting to find a tray of food. I do, but it's accompanied by Maksim's smiling face. He nods into the room, and I open the door wider, allowing him in. He sets the tray on the dresser and peeks under the stainless steel lid.

I say loudly enough for Maksim to hear, "I need to run. My dinner just arrived."

"Report back to me when you get back," Mr. Gerhardt orders.

"Will do."

"Have a good night, Paisley."

The call dies, and I tuck my phone in the back pocket of my jeans.

"Who was that?" Maksim asks.

"Your boss," I say

His eyebrows shoot up. "He pissed about the flipping off situation?" His back falls to the mattress and he stares at the ceiling.

"Of course. What were you thinking?" I'm slightly pissed myself, because I know he can control himself better than that.

"I wasn't thinking. I was pissed, which is why I'm here."

I cross my arms. "You shouldn't be here. Someone might have seen you."

"You're ruining me," he says.

"What?"

"I want you so bad it aches. I thought I could do it. I mean, I have the kind of willpower it would take to push you out of my mind, but damn, you're too much. You won't leave my head." He sits back up.

I stare blankly, unsure how to respond. No man has ever said anything like that to me.

"You barely know me."

"And I want to get to know you. I want to know everything."

I shake my head. For a brief moment, I was enamored by what he was saying. "You mean you want to know what kind of panties I wear. If I'm loud when I come and if I like dirty talk in bed. Those are the things you're thinking about."

"Fuck yeah, I do."

I nod, pleased with myself that I was correct.

"But I also want to know why you picked a pretzel over nachos today. And why you ordered a salad with grilled chicken right now. And I fucking love that you ordered dessert even though you tried for a nutritious dinner."

"Because I have a sweet tooth. It's not unique."

"Still, what's your favorite dessert?"

I shake my head. "I have a lot."

"I'm not really asking. I want to discover all this stuff by being with you. All the small things that make you, you. Do I want to have sex with you? I do. But I also want all of you. Your thoughts, your fears, your desires and pet peeves. Everything."

I walk toward the window, turning my back to Maksim so I can clear my thoughts. He's too gorgeous for me to not fall to my knees and beg him to take me. But he'll only hurt me. I know it. "How many girls do you take back to your room in a season?"

"Is that where your reluctancy is coming? You think I say this to every girl?"

I shrug, not turning around.

"I've never had a shittier season with the amount of time I've been in the penalty box. Ever since I met you, I haven't been myself."

"You have no idea if it's me or not." I continue to look at the dark sky of Toronto and the city glittering out for miles below.

"When I was skating down the ice tonight, I was searching you out. I know you saw me."

I did, but a guy like Maksim Petrov knows how to woo a woman. He's not a stranger to going with gusto after what he wants and getting it. And there's something appealing about that. Something that makes me want to say yes to tonight. To cross that line with him and allow him to show me how a woman should feel in bed with a man. Give me the kind of orgasms I hear other women talk about. The only question that needs answering is whether I can walk out of here tomorrow morning without developing any feelings for him because that's all we could ever be—a one-and-done.

"I'd have to refer you to someone else," I whisper, afraid of the thoughts going through my head. Am I really thinking about doing this?

"I signed that paper and I meant it." The bed squeaks from his weight lifting off of it. "I don't need therapy anyway."

I blow out a breath and tighten my arms around myself. His hands land on my shoulders and my eyes drift closed.

"Why are you fighting so hard against this?" he whispers.

His aftershave hits my nostrils, filling me with the same feeling I had on New Year's Eve. That kiss felt so magical, as if I was warped into some fairy tale, only for me to open my eyes to a nightmare as though Mr. Gerhardt was my wicked stepmother.

Take this, Paisley. Take something for yourself and to hell with the consequences for once.

I circle around and his hands fall to my hips.

"You're so fucking stunning," he says, his eyes pouring affection over me like lava, slow and hot.

"You don't have to keep complimenting me. You're going to get what you want tonight." I raise on my tiptoes and close my eyes just before my lips press against… a stubbled cheek? What the heck?

I open my eyes and fall back down on my heels. Maksim turns his head back to me. I've never seen this look before.

"What does that mean?" His sweet syrupy voice turns cool.

"You want to have sex and I'm saying okay."

He steps back. "That's not what this is about, Paisley. It's not just sex."

I roll my eyes. "You don't have to put on an act. I know exactly why you're in my hotel room. I'm flattered to make the cut, and you're right, I'm attracted to you."

He shakes his head, shoving his hands into his pockets. "You still think you're just some piece of ass for me."

I walk over and sit on the bed. "I've been around hockey guys most of my life. Sure, there are some good ones out there, but most just want sex. Don't act like your pride is hurt because I'm calling you out on it. I said okay. You're finally getting what you want." I grab the hem of my shirt and tear it off over my head.

"What are you doing?"

"I'm giving you what you want. Why are you acting all noble now?"

His hands go into his hair. "What the hell is happening right now?"

"That's my question. Shouldn't I be on my third orgasm by now?"

His eyes narrow. "What the hell happened to you?"

I'm growing irritated that he's not kissing me yet. He's the one who's been pursuing me. Why is he being difficult now?

"Put your shirt back on."

"Why?" I stretch out on the bed. "I'm making this easier on you."

He comes over to the bed and his finger winds around

one of my curls. "I don't want you like this. I want to date you. Like I said—"

"And you also want to sleep with me, correct?" All that other stuff he said was bullshit, so why won't he just get down with what I'm offering?

"Yes. More than anything. Except for showing you I'm not the guy you think I am." He picks up my shirt and shoves the opening over my head.

I huff and my mouth drops open. "You're denying me?"

"Yes."

"Way to make a girl feel wanted."

He takes my hand and places it between his legs. "This should tell you everything you need to know, but I'm walking away anyway. I'm going back to my room and I'm going to bed. You'll figure it out soon enough that I'm not just blowing smoke up your ass, *kotik*."

His dick is half hard and big. Like *really* big. Damn, maybe I shouldn't have called him out on his bullshit. Maybe if I hadn't, he'd already be rocking inside me, filling me. I suck in a breath, thinking about that. My hand drops to my lap as he walks toward the door.

"You've got great tits, by the way. I would've devoured them." He opens the door and leaves.

I fall down to the mattress. What the hell just happened?

---

*A*fter I've sulked for a while, I grab my phone and dial up Jana, tearing the lid off the chocolate cake from room service.

"What's up?" she answers.

"You're never going to believe what just happened." I

go through everything from how flirtatious Maksim was being to what just happened when he left my room. Then I shove a forkful of cake in my mouth.

"Why were you going to just do it?" she asks.

"Because he's hot, and I was finally rewarding myself with a one night with a hockey god."

"Like a birthday gift?" She laughs.

"Exactly."

"Nothing wrong with that except he flipped the script on you." She sounds amused.

"Yes! I was going to be a willing participant," I mumble around another mouthful.

A very willing participant.

"Maybe he's one of those guys who just like the chase, you know? Then when you finally said yes, he bailed. Although I will say that from what I know of Maksim, that doesn't sound like him."

I sulk down in bed. Jana's right. Most of the time when Maksim is mentioned in the press, it's because he's removing Ford from a bad situation.

"Now I have to get on a plane with him tomorrow."

"Just ignore him. I'm kind of pissed he's playing you like this. I mean, going after you full force and then acting like he has no interest." She's quiet for a minute. "Hey, Paise?"

"What?"

"Do you *like* Maksim Petrov?"

I love Jana, but if I answer honestly, she's going to insert herself in the situation. Either by cornering Maksim and playing the juvenile game of "do you like my friend," or worse, she'll scold him for leaving me high and wet— definitely not dry.

So rather than admitting I can't stop thinking about

him, I say, "I don't know. He's attractive and seems almost sweet sometimes."

"I'm not sure anyone has referred to Maksim as sweet," she says.

"Attentive maybe. But… errgghhh!" I just don't know what to think after tonight.

"Well, if he's going to act so hot and cold, just ignore him, Paise. Move on. Do the rest of the therapy sessions and forget him after that. You know, my dad mentioned at dinner tonight about fixing you up with someone."

My eyes widen. "What? I don't want to be fixed up."

This isn't the first time Mr. Gerhardt has tried to fix me up. For some reason, he always picks accountants or men with equally boring jobs. Men who have played it safe all their lives and wear three-piece suits to work. And there's nothing wrong with those guys. They're the ones you marry for stability, but I'm too young to marry anyone, and for some dumb reason, I have this stupid idea that I want to be with a more rough-and-tumble guy. Someone who knows his way around a woman. And because I know that kind of guy isn't what's good for me, my sex life is left in a stalemate.

Jana interrupts my thoughts. "Just be on the lookout and dodge Dad if you see him."

"I will."

I hang up with Jana a few minutes later. All I can think about is how Maksim is the kind of guy I'm attracted to and how that long, hard dick I felt might be exactly what I need to get me out of my rut. I try to ease the ache between my thighs, but alas, I think there's only one person who can.

CHAPTER 9

"Oh, sweet kotik."

Maksim

*L*ater that week, after practice, there's a note in my locker.

See Mr. Gerhardt ASAP

Blyat. I tear it off the wall, crumple it, and toss it in the trash.

"Two points." Ford raises two fingers and heads into the shower with a bunch of my other teammates.

I sit on the bench and unlace my skates.

"What's that about?" Aiden asks.

"Gerhardt wants to see me." I groan and take off my skates and socks. "Probably because of the game."

Last night we had a home game, and I might've crossed the line when a guy on the other team tripped Ford and he almost went crashing headfirst into the boards. You can paralyze a player doing shit like that, and of course, the refs didn't see it. So I went after Klein from behind to return the favor and was suspended for the rest of the game.

"I'm not sure why he's so up your ass lately," Aiden says, taking off his pads.

"Me either. I'm not doing anything different than before."

Aiden cocks an eyebrow.

"Okay, maybe I'm a little more aggressive out there," I say.

"Does it have anything to do with a certain brunette?"

I remove my own pads. "No. I mean, I might be sexually frustrated because I do want her, but my job is to protect my guys, and what Klein did to Ford was bullshit. Right? I'm not seeing things."

Aiden hems and haws. "It was bullshit, and yeah, you've always had our backs. Kept me from being double-teamed ever since we both started playing for the Fury, but…"

"What?"

He sits on the bench and rests his forearms on his thighs. "You know even the Florida Fury fans are making up nicknames for you?"

My eyes narrow. "Like?"

"I mean, I think they want them to be endearing. They still love you, of course. But do you want to be known as Mad Reaper or Psycho Cobra?"

"What kind of names are those?" Those suck. They don't even sound like hockey nicknames.

"Exactly. You gotta control yourself out there. Maybe talking to Paisley is the way to go. Get your head straight." Aiden wraps a towel around himself.

"I don't need therapy. I'm just trying to make sure people leave you the hell alone."

He puts his hand on my shoulder. "It's not all on you, man. Why do you think that?"

I've never told a soul about Armen. When I came to the United States, I decided to leave all that shit back in Russia, but since all this therapy talk has come up, Armen's been in my head late at night when I'm lying in bed. The car crash unfolds in my head in slow motion. His parents' faces when they heard the news. Nadiya crumbling and sobbing.

I shrug off Aiden and stand, wrapping my own towel around my waist. "Maybe because you assholes are too big of pussies to protect yourselves." I laugh and walk toward the showers.

"You better watch yourself after that comment."

By the time we hit the showers, we're laughing and the seriousness of the moment has passed. Thank God.

***

A half hour later, I'm waiting outside Gerhardt's office. His secretary is giving me the evil eye over her computer screen. She's old enough to be Gerhardt's mother, but those rumors were squashed after someone discovered that his mother lived in Boca Raton with live-in caregivers until she passed two years ago.

Mrs. Turner wears librarian glasses—the ones attached to a chain—and her scowl is scarier than mine. She's the complete opposite of who you'd think would manage Gerhardt's daily schedule.

Gerhardt's voice comes over the speaker of Mrs. Turner's phone. "Send him in."

Mrs. Turner widens her beady little eyes as if I'm on death row and about to meet my maker.

"Always a pleasure," I say to her, walking through the double oak doors into Gerhardt's office. I stop in my tracks when I see Paisley on the couch.

What the fuck?

Did she rat me out after last week in Toronto when I redressed her and left her in bed?

It was the hardest decision of my life, but I'm not going to sleep with someone who's clearly waiting for me to hurt her. As though I'm the typical athlete you see on television, getting into public fights with their spouse or openly cheating on them. I would never hurt someone like that. Have I had sex with a bunny? Sure. But there wasn't anyone at home waiting for me either.

"If it isn't the Grim Reaper himself." Gerhardt's angry tone is hard to miss.

"I hear it's the Mad Reaper," I say, which is the wrong move because Gerhardt motions to the couch cushion next to Paisley.

"Sit, Petrov."

I do as I'm told because although the trade deadline has passed, he could get rid of me at the end of this season, and I like my boys and living in Florida. Nadiya needs to stay in Florida for school, so I can't jeopardize that either.

"Mad just makes you sound psychotic," Gerhardt says, picking up his drink and spinning it around before sipping it. "I asked you both in here because I was just informed of something."

Paisley's hands are clenched so tightly, her knuckles are white. I'd do about anything to grab one and hold it to tell her it will all be all right. I can't deny my own heart is racing while I try to figure out who could've ratted us out.

"What's that?" Paisley's voice is soft and innocent, so I'll let her run this show how she sees fit.

"This therapy thing isn't working as we planned. I've seen no improvement in your behavior on the ice." He eyes me over the rim of his glass.

"Therapy isn't a Band-Aid, Mr. Gerhardt. It takes time, but…" She glances at me and turns back to Gerhardt. "I'd like to suggest that Maksim sees someone else."

Gerhardt waves her off. "No, it's not you. You're more than capable." He smiles at her. They really do have a close relationship. He directs his attention to me. "There's work to do to make sure your image with the fans stays intact. Everyone loves the hothead to a certain point, but they need to get a sense of you off the ice as well."

My forehead wrinkles. "Excuse me?"

"Florida Fury fans love you. They love how you protect your boys out there, but things have gone too far lately. This guy, Ike Breaner, called me today looking for a sponsor for an at-risk youth hockey team he works with. They need some money to run the team and some coaches to help them with their game."

"That's very nice of you, Mr. Gerhardt," Paisley says.

"I hope you still think that when I tell you that I'd like you two to head it up."

Paisley coughs and reaches for a bottle of water that's sitting in front of her.

Interesting. But if I can somehow use this as a tradeoff for therapy, I'm down.

"I know you're both busy and Petrov won't be able to be as involved as you, Paisley, because of his commitments to the team, but from the amount of time you hang out with Jana, it seems you have time to kill."

She scoffs quietly, and I bite down my laugh at Gerhardt pretty much saying she doesn't have a social life except for her best friend. I'm more than happy to find out she doesn't date much.

"Well, I do have other clients besides the team," she says.

He nods. "I know you do, but you don't see them on the weekends, do you?"

"What exactly are we required to do?" I ask.

Gerhardt sighs, stands, and refills his glass. "I wouldn't

think of it as a requirement. It should be fun. Sure, you're both there representing the Fury, but this will also let people see another side of you, Petrov." He sits in his chair across from the couch. "You two would coach them—Paisley being the head coach, because of your time constrictions."

Paisley almost spits out her water but manages to swallow it. Bad visuals accost my brain for a moment before I get my act together. "Did you say I'm the head coach?"

Gerhardt nods. "I have every confidence you'll do a fine job."

"Mr. Gerhardt, I've never played hockey. I just enjoy watching it."

"And you know your stuff as well as any of the guys on the team. How many conversations have we had about plays and strategies?"

"A lot," she murmurs.

Interesting.

"And what do you expect me to do?" I ask.

He turns in my direction while Paisley stares into her lap. So far, she hasn't glanced at me once.

"You'll be the one on the ice, helping to develop their skills. I'd like you guys to make the schedule around the games so you're there as much as possible. This will be great for you. The Fury fans are going to love you."

I thought they already did.

He takes a file folder off the table and slides it over to us. "Here you go. This is all the information you need. I'll be at your first game."

We both stare at the folder. He can't seriously demand for me to do this. I mean, Paisley will do it out of the goodness of her heart, but me? My focus should be on hockey. Why is he always trying to control me?

"Can I speak to you a moment?" I say to Mr. Gerhardt.

"I know what you're going to say. You need to do this, Maksim. For both our sakes." His tone makes it clear this isn't really a request.

Paisley picks up the file folder and thumbs through it. She'll do this whether I involve myself or not. She's too kindhearted to tell Gerhardt to shove it up his ass, that if he wants everyone to think of him as some great guy who gives to the youth, then his ass should be out there with the kids. And I want to. I want to tell him off so bad right now, but Paisley won't.

So for her sake, I nod and say, "I'm in."

Gerhardt's slimy smile almost makes me retract that declaration, but I don't.

"Good. Now the two of you can go discuss it. Figure out a schedule that works for both of you." He heads over to his desk.

Paisley stands. "Thank you, Mr. Gerhardt."

"Oh no, thank you, Paisley. If you need anything, just let me know. Jana said something about wanting to design the jerseys."

Paisley nods, but from the look on her face, I'm guessing that's not going to happen.

"Get your act together, Petrov," he says.

I close my eyes, thinking of my parents and Nadiya and all the friends I've made here. I can't keep pissing off the boss and expect him to keep me here.

"Sure." I wave and walk out the doors of the office.

We both bypass Mrs. Turner's desk as she snickers to herself. Once we're in the hallway, Paisley heads to her office and I follow, but she shuts the door in my face. Without missing a beat, I open the door and step inside.

Her back is to me and she's looking over the paperwork. God, her ass in that skirt is delectable.

My hands clench at my sides, wanting to squeeze it. "Paisley?"

She holds up her hand. "I've got this handled. We can just pretend, like we did with the therapy."

"But—"

She turns around, and the sweet woman I've fallen for has disappeared. "It's okay, Maksim. I'm a big girl."

I walk over and take the folder from her grasp. "This is my responsibility too. You're not going to do this by yourself."

She grabs it back, almost giving me a paper cut. "I think it's better if we keep our distance from each other."

"Distance?" I stare at her, stepping forward until I'm centimeters away from her and my hands rest on the desk behind her. "You want distance?"

"Well, you did leave me shirtless in a hotel room last weekend."

I chuckle. Is that what this attitude is about? I was doing the right thing. "I dressed you before I left if I remember correctly."

She's quiet for a beat. "Should I thank you for only partially embarrassing me?"

"Oh, sweet *kotik.*" I inch my hands closer to her hips and her breathing shallows.

"What does that mean? You called me that before." Her voice is labored.

"It means kitten." Her forehead wrinkles, and I say, "Because you're cute and innocent looking like a kitten, but you have claws."

Her eyes widen. I think she likes my pet name for her.

"Anyway, I simply had to make a point."

"And what point were you making?" she asks.

"That I'm not some player you can screw one time and be done with."

She stares at me for a long beat, then she laughs. Laughs so hard, my own mood improves. That's when I know I'm in too deep.

CHAPTER 10

"That's a lot to ask."

Paisley

One week later, I arrive at the Fury arena with a box of supplies to start the at-risk youth program. We're going to be called the Fury Juniors and Jana has agreed to help me.

"Hey, Sid, thanks for coming in," I say to the security guard who has to be here on overtime to watch over the building during our practice.

"No problem, Miss Paisley."

Mr. Gerhardt pulled out all the stops to make sure these kids feel like royalty. He hired a bus to pick them up and bring them here. They each have new skates, pads, and jerseys that Jana designed. Not sure how a bunch of twelve-year-olds will feel about polar bears, but it is what it is.

I'm just getting everything organized when Jana walks in. I raise my eyebrows at her and she stops, looking down at herself.

"What are you wearing?" I ask, shaking my head.

She has on pink spandex tights, a leotard, leg warmers, and a pair of brand-new white skates hanging from her shoulder. She holds her arms out to her sides. "What?"

"The eighties called and you're wanted in Jazzercise."

She narrows her eyes.

Seriously, I maybe could have understood if she showed up in a sequin leotard like when she was in the midst of her figure skating obsession, but I'm not sure where she got this look from.

"I see nothing wrong with this," she says. "I need to be flexible."

"All the twelve-year-olds are going to be staring at your ass the entire time."

She turns around and wiggles her ass in my direction, then picks up one of the jerseys. "Oh, it turned out so cute. Don't you think it's cute?"

"It's cute," I say because it is, and I know she meant well.

She sits on a bench and looks around. The Zamboni just cleaned the ice and it gleams in shiny perfection. "Where's your sidekick?"

"I told you, I have it under control. He needs to worry about other things."

"I don't think that's your call to make."

I ignore her comment until I have everyone's stuff out for them, then I join Jana. "I'm way too embarrassed to continue seeing him. We have one more therapy session— if we're going to consider the first two legit, which they weren't. And that stays between us."

She holds out her pinkie and I wrap mine around it.

"You have nothing to be embarrassed about."

Jana has told me that multiple times, but I don't believe her.

"I took off my shirt, offered myself up on a silver platter, and he ran out of the room as fast as he could." I haven't told her that he complimented my breasts, but I guess that's the least he could've done.

"Relax, maybe you two are playing some game. It's his form of foreplay or something."

"I don't do games," I say.

Her head bobbles. I love my best friend, but she's never had a guy tell her no. It stings, to put it mildly.

We hear the kids before we see them step through the opening into the arena. Each of them has wide eyes and their mouths hanging open as they look at all the seats, the Jumbotron, the ice.

"Man," one kid says. "I can't believe this."

Another kid hits the first kid on the chest with his forearm. "You know there's a catch. They're using us to look good."

A girl with braids on either side of her head pushes between them. "Who the hell cares? Use me all you want. This is amazing." She turns to me, but her gaze shifts to the bench where everything is laid out. "Holy crap, is that for us?"

All the other kids take notice and they each run, finding the set with their name on the back of the jersey.

The girl with braids looks at me. "Like, these are for us?"

I nod. "Hi, I'm Paisley."

None of them introduce themselves, too enthralled with everything. Maybe I went about this all wrong.

"Hello!" Jana screams. "She introduced herself."

All the kids look at her.

The first boy who came in stares her up and down. "Where did you come from?"

"My dreams," the other boy says.

"I like your outfit, where can I get one?" a different girl, who's now next to the one with braids, asks.

"Really?" Jana asks, giving me a look over their shoulder like 'I told you so.' "Well—"

Both girls laugh. "No."

Jana's smile dims, but I know she has mirrors in her house. Then again, she gets away with a lot of the fashion chances she takes—just not this one.

I run my hand over Jana's arm to soothe her ego. Kids are straightforward. Then I clap to try to gain their attention. They all turn in my direction for a moment, but quickly return to conversations of their own.

"Okay, quiet down," I say. I don't have a teacher's voice though. I have a soothing psychologist's voice and it's not getting me anywhere with these kids. "Please have a seat."

Still nothing. Jana purses her lips, watching the kids ignore me.

"Kids!" I say in the loudest voice I have, but it still lacks the authority I need.

"Sit down!" Jana yells.

All the kids look at her.

The first kid who walked in raises his eyebrows at her. "Calm down, Jane Fonda."

"Who the hell is Jane Fonda?" a red-haired kid asks.

"My mom found her video tapes at the Salvation Army and she's doing them every day. She dresses just like her," one of the girls says.

Jana's bottom lip trembles before anger replaces it. I laugh at my best friend. I know a lot of trends have come back, but I don't think leotards with spandex and leg warmers have. Maybe she's starting something though.

"Your mom doesn't need to work out. She's got an amazing ass," another kid says.

"Okay, that's enough chitchatting," I say. "Sit down so we can go over what we're going to do today."

They listen this time and sit on the bench.

"We were told the Fury players were gonna be here,"

the girl in braids says. "You two definitely aren't them. Is he?" She thumbs toward Sid.

Sid might be able to pass for a retired hockey player.

"No. That's Sid, he's with security."

The red-haired kid leans into the first kid. "He's here to make sure we don't steal anything."

"That is not what I meant." I give the kid a stern look, but he's not concerned about me.

"Then why is he here? To help us in case you go mental?" the red-haired kid asks.

Jana shakes her head. "Just be quiet and listen to her. This is ridiculous."

When they finally quiet down, I introduce myself again. "I'm Paisley Pearce, and I'm your coach. This is Jana, and she's going to assist me."

"Assist us in learning twirls?" the girl in braids asks.

"No, she knows how to skate. How many of you know how to skate?"

Half of them raise their hands.

"And out of you, how comfortable are you in skates?"

Half of them wave their hands back and forth. Oh boy, do I have my work cut out for me. Then again, we're in Florida. I don't know why I expected any different.

"That's fine. I just wanted to know where to start. We'll work on skating first. Let's do some introductions so I know who everyone is." I point at the first kid who came in.

"Malcolm," the kid says.

The red-haired kid says, "Dru."

"Meaning Drew, as in Andrew," Malcolm corrects him.

"It's D.R.U."

The group rolls their eyes.

"Okay, Dru." I continue down the line.

The girl in braids speaks up. "I'm Lark."

"And I'm Marin," the other girl says.

They're the only two girls in the group, and I can already tell that they're probably going to be the toughest.

"Great. Each of you have your jerseys. If you want to just put them over your shirts, then we can get your skates on."

After Jana and I work tirelessly to get all their laces done up tightly enough on their skates, I'm already exhausted and I haven't even helped them to stand on their skates.

"Jana is going to show you the basics of skating."

Jana opens up the door and glides out onto the ice.

"Man, I'd learn to figure skate just to put my hands on her thighs in a lift," Dru says.

"You watch figure skating?" Lark gives him a judgmental glare.

"Um, there are half-naked women on there. I'm not ashamed."

"Let's focus on her footwork," I say. "Look how she shifts her weight from one leg and pushes off with the opposite one."

"That's a lot to ask, Miss Paisley," Dru says, and I'm pretty sure his eyes are fixed on Jana's ass and not her footwork.

"Where are the Fury players? I want to learn to hit," Malcolm chimes in, looking around.

"I can probably get a few here one day, but for the most part, it's just going to be Jana and me."

They groan.

"You're going to teach us how to hit a puck in the net?" Dru asks skeptically, looking at Malcolm as though we're from Mars.

Jana stops herself on the edge of the wall instead of using her skates. So maybe she's not as good as she was once. "See how much fun this is?"

"Use a stick and a puck." Marin grabs a stick, hands it over the boards to Jana, then throws the puck on the ice.

"Sure." Jana gives me a fleeting look of terror but takes the stick and hits the puck. She's clearly unable to control the puck because she's chasing it more than anything.

The kids all watch her, some groaning, others sighing, and the rest looking on with disbelief. I imagine they all had high hopes, and now I feel like shit for taking away their opportunity to learn from a Fury player because I was too embarrassed to face him.

I'm a giver. I've always been a giver, and yeah, sometimes that's gotten me into trouble. Gotten my heart broken. For instance, when I gave my dad a chance at fifteen—after he said he wanted to have a relationship with me—only for his new wife to tell him he couldn't take me on a trip to Paris when she'd yet to go there herself. And that's only one instance.

After today, I'm going to have to suck up my pride and ask Maksim to help me with these kids. But right now, they're here and we need to make the most of it.

I grab the skate trainers that slide along the ice to help them learn. "Everyone, take one of these and make your way to the ice. Use these until you feel comfortable."

They listen to me and venture out onto the ice. Some of their ankles buckle, but each of them seems to have a perseverance that's admirable. Dru follows Jana around as if she's a supermodel, and the girls laugh together while they find their footing. Malcolm falls and his walker slides away from him, leaving him helpless on the ice. All the kids glance over and look at each other uncomfortably as he crawls over to the door leading to the bench.

Malcolm pulls off his helmet and tosses it across the way. "This is so stupid. I'm ready to leave."

As the kids all start venturing off the ice, one thing

becomes clear—Malcolm is their leader. Whatever he says goes. Even Dru holds on for life as he makes his way over to his friend. He mumbles how right Malcolm is, that this is lame and wondering why they even bothered coming.

I'm about to lose them and I feel terrible. Also, how the hell am I going to explain this to Mr. Gerhardt?

CHAPTER 11

Maksim

I watch from the team hallway to the arena. I should save Paisley. The kids want to see a Fury team member and they were promised one. But that day in her office when she laughed, she also put her hand on my chest and pushed me away, saying she had it under control and that my presence wasn't necessary—or wanted.

The kid is embarrassed that he fell, and from what I gather, he's the leader of their group. How he reacts, what he does, will be what the others follow. So I'm not surprised to see the rest of them getting off the ice in comradery with their friend.

I look down at my jean-clad legs and skates. I need to just skate out there and take control whether Paisley wants me here or not.

She looks at the ceiling and her eyes close for a moment. Jana comes up next to her, putting her hand on Paisley's back.

Yeah, fuck it, I'm going in.

I walk out, open the door to the ice, and glide out with my stick in hand. Without granting them any attention, I hit the puck Jana pitifully tried to handle. I do a few fancy tricks, nothing crazy, then backhand the puck into the goal.

When I skate around, all the kids are watching me in

awe. Gotta say, I never tire of that look. I switch my focus to Paisley. She's wearing the slightest of smiles, but I know there's gratitude there. I'm doing my best to respect her boundaries, but sometimes people get in their own way.

"Hey, guys," I say.

"Maksim Petrov?" the kid who made a spectacle of himself says.

I nod.

"How did you do that?" he asks.

"It's easy, I could do that," the red-haired kid says, and all the kids disagree in unison. "It didn't look that hard."

I hold out my stick for him. "Want to give it a try?"

"Well, um…"

I smile. I like the kid's confidence though.

"Want to see another one?" I ask.

"Yeah!" they all scream.

"I'll need Miss Paisley to come and assist me."

Paisley's already shaking her head. "I don't know how to skate."

The girl in braids holds out a stick to her.

"Then let me teach you." I skate over to the opening, holding out my hand.

All the kids cheer her on. She must realize she has no chance of declining in front of the kids because she takes my hand. I accept the stick from the girl in braids, holding both in my one hand while I clench Paisley's hand with my other so she doesn't fall on the ice.

"I'm not any good," she whispers once we're in the middle of the ice.

"It will do them good to see you fall. Make them understand this isn't easy and they're not going to get it their first time," I tell her. A whiff of her perfume floats up to my nostrils and all I can think about is how she looked in her bra that night, lying on the hotel room bed.

"Maybe you should be the one who falls," she says.

I shrug. "I'm the one they look up to."

Being unable to stop on her skates, she falls right into me. Her soft breasts press against my hard chest. "Exactly."

"Okay, okay. But I'll have to do some move that's crazy skilled before that happens."

She laughs.

We skate around the oval once, and when she's a little steadier on her skates, I hand her the stick. "Ready?"

Although she looks as though she might throw up, she nods. I love how determined she is. I'm easy on her, me skating backward and her forward toward me.

"Just glide toward me slowly. I'm here if you fall," I softly say so it's only us who can hear.

"GO, PAISE!" Jana screams.

"GO, MAKSIM!" the boys chant.

"Keep coming." I pretend to get the puck, but she hunkers down and slaps the stick on the ice, getting it away.

Since she has no shot, I grab the puck and move it between us again.

"Thanks," she says.

"You're going to be the one that scores," I tell her and she shakes her head.

"Listen to me. All you have to do is skate closer to me, get the puck in the middle of the stick, knock it to the right, and pick up the stick and place it on the other side, knocking it left, and it will go right into the goal."

"You're kidding me, right? I can barely stand up straight in these skates, let alone direct a puck."

"I got you." I wink.

For a moment, it's only us here. There aren't a bunch of little eyes watching our every move.

"You better have me," she says.

"Trust me." I meet her gaze, and she gives me a quick nod. "Okay, ready. Set. Go."

She directs the puck and lifts the stick just in time. When she hits it to go into the net, she doesn't hit it hard enough, so as I pretend skate to stop the puck from going in, I give it a little tap and the buzzer goes off. Everyone cheers.

"Let's see your celly," I say.

"Celly?"

"Your celebration move after scoring."

Paisley stops skating, holds on to the edge, then claps.

I shake my head. "That's no celly, am I right?" I yell over to the kids.

"No!" they holler back.

I skate over, dropping my stick, and pick her up and skate her around the ice. "Raise your hands and celebrate."

She does, and her smile is so genuine and pure, my heart aches, wishing it were for me. I set her down back where we started.

"You did this so you could touch me, didn't you?" she whispers.

I shrug. "You'll never know. Come and introduce me to the kids."

I take her hand and we skate over to the group, her releasing my hand immediately once we get there.

"Very impressive," Jana says.

"She did great."

Paisley rolls her eyes but starts the introductions. "This is Maksim Petrov, for those of you who don't know. He's the defenseman for the Florida Fury."

"My mom says you're scary," Marin says.

"I love it when you fight," Dru chimes in.

"And when you sprayed water on that one fan who wouldn't leave you alone? Awesome," another kid whose name I didn't catch says.

"Glad you like the way I play, but my job as a defenseman is to help out my goalie. Have his back, plus protect my center and wingmen. Sometimes fights are necessary to make sure they know I'm watching."

"Will you teach us to skate like that?" Dru asks.

"Please, this is stupid. When are we ever going to do this outside of a rink?" Malcolm says. "We live in Florida, not the North Pole."

Dru looks at his friend. "True."

"Yeah, he's from Russia. He was probably born with skates," the girl I think is Lark says.

"Well, that would've hurt my mom," I joke, but I can see I'm losing them, so I set my eyes on Malcolm. "Give me ten minutes."

"Ten minutes for what?" he grumbles.

"In ten minutes, you'll be able to skate around the rink. Maybe nothing fancy, but you'll be able to skate."

He waves me off. "Whatever."

"Are you afraid?" I pin him with a stare.

Dru's eyes widen. But I know that a kid who acts like Malcolm will back down when someone says he might be afraid.

"No. I just think this whole thing is stupid," Malcolm says.

"Fair enough. Feel free to sit out. How about you, Dru? Ten minutes?"

Dru looks at his friend and bites his lip. "Nah, man, I'm here." He sits down next to Malcolm.

"I'm game!" Lark raises her hand.

"What the hell?" Dru says.

Lark looks at Dru and Dru eyes Malcolm. "If he wants

to sit there and act tough, I don't care, but we're here and will probably never have the chance to learn from someone like him again." She comes out to the ice, holding on to the side.

"Okay, Lark. Hold my hands."

She puts hers in mine. She wobbles a bit, but she doesn't let go, instead getting a look of determination on her face.

"You skate forward, I skate backward, and I'll help you balance." I start skating and she follows me. "One foot and then the other." At first, she's trying to walk. "Glide. Push off with one foot."

Ten minutes later, we're all watching Lark skate on her own. Sure, she loses her balance once in a while and looks like she might fall backward, but she's doing it and I'm damn proud of her.

"Anyone else?" Paisley asks.

"Me." Marin comes out with me and picks it up quicker than her friend did. Five minutes later, she joins Lark, the two of them skating side by side.

After that, most of the kids come out and ask to learn. Our time is about to end and only Dru and Malcolm are still on the bench, pretending they're bored. I decide to give it another shot, leaving Paisley and Jana to manage the group on the ice.

"When I was little, I was afraid to skate. Sure, I was a lot younger than you, but I'd go on the weekends and watch my dad skate in a men's league. Some of the guys would leave with blood gushing out of their mouths and broken noses. The game was much rougher then than how it's played now. Maybe that's because it was Russia." I shrug. "But my friend Armen told me he wouldn't do it if I didn't do it. He picked it up immediately, while I didn't. I just couldn't get the hang of gliding and would always end up face-first on the ice or in a snow pile because I couldn't stop."

"And?" Malcolm asks with an attitude and bravado only a kid his age can have without getting beat up.

"And one day he took me to a pond and taught me everything he knew without anyone watching."

"So?" Malcolm says.

"So I'm willing to do that for you."

"Who said we want to?" Dru asks.

"I'm not an idiot. We both know you guys want to get out there, but you're saving face. I'm only offering this once. Next time you guys are here, I'll make sure it's just you two and me on the ice for a bit. None of your friends here to see anything. What do you say?"

I can't tell if they're thinking it over. Dru looks at Malcolm. It's clear he's going to be the decision-maker on this.

"Last chance…" I cross my arms.

Malcolm nods and shrugs. "Okay."

"And you?" I ask Dru.

He nods and smiles widely. "Hell yeah."

"Okay then. But there's no giving up, got it? When you leave here, you'll know how to skate."

They both agree, then the bus driver and chaperone come in to get the kids. We say goodbye, and after they're gone, Jana says she's going to change. I want to say she should've done that a long time ago, but I'm smart enough to keep my mouth shut.

Paisley and I sit beside each other on the bench. She bends over and struggles to untie her skates. "I guess I owe you a thank you for showing up anyway."

I grab her leg and put it over my lap, then work the laces loose. "You just had to let me be a part of it in the first place."

I slowly slide the skate off her foot and set it down before doing the same thing with the other one.

"I was embarrassed, Maksim. I offered myself to you only to be turned down."

I sigh. "I didn't turn you down."

"Yes, you did."

I shake my head. "I only turned down a one-night stand."

"What?" She wiggles her toes.

I take her right foot in my hands and massage it. "I don't want only one night with you, *kotik*, and I'm going to prove I'm not that type of guy. I don't take relationships lightly. I'm drawn to you like no one before you, and yeah, I want to sleep with you so bad my dick is throwing tantrums every day, but I'll beat off to my imagination until I convince you I'm not the guy you've typecast me as."

She sighs and slides her legs off my lap. "It's not that easy. I was hurt by the first man I ever loved, and I know all men aren't like that. I know there are good men out there and I have no doubt you're one of them. But it's still here." She presses her hand to her heart. "Some scars refuse to heal."

I place my hand over hers. "Give me one shot. Dinner. Tonight?"

She takes so long to answer, I fear maybe she won't, but then it's there, so small and so soft I almost miss it. "Okay."

I exhale a sigh of relief. Now I just have to pull out the red carpet and plan one helluva date with hardly any notice. I've done harder things.

CHAPTER 12

"Tell me one thing..."

Paisley

"**D**id he say where he wants to take you?" Jana asks on speaker as I search my closet for something to wear. I should have gone over to Jana's place. She has endless options.

"Nope. Best guess, restaurant and a movie. Or maybe just dinner, no movie? Italian restaurant maybe. Then I'll want to order the spaghetti, but a first date and spaghetti… you might as well say you don't want a second date."

Jana laughs. "Something tells me Maksim isn't going to care how you eat spaghetti."

"Then I'll end up getting some kind of salad, and I'll come home and eat cereal after because I'm starving."

She laughs again. "You think too much."

"Because I'm not the gorgeous blonde across the table from them like you."

She's silent for a moment. "I hate it when you do that to yourself."

"I'm not down on myself. These are facts. You're gorgeous and I'm the girl next door. And there's nothing wrong with the girl next door. I'll probably marry some good-looking insurance guy who will take me for Italian dinners and always remember our anniversary." What I don't say to Jana is that he'll probably let me run the house and make corny jokes like, "happy wife, happy life."

"You don't sound like that's what you want."

"Because it's not. I want someone who challenges me. Who will fight with me until we end up having hot sex on the floor and he pulls my hair back and drills into me from behind."

"Man, I think our friendship just took a turn." She laughs. "Tell me more, sex kitten."

I flop down on my bed, still in my robe. "You can't tell me you'd want some guy who treats you like a porcelain doll."

"No. Definitely not. And I know you're probably going to think I'm boring, but I like missionary."

"I didn't say there's anything wrong with missionary. I just don't want to be staring up at the ceiling every night, faking an orgasm and pretending to enjoy his sweaty body on top of me."

"Paisley!" she yells and cackles with laughter.

"What?" I chuckle.

"I never knew any of this about you."

I sigh. "Well, now you do. But I'm either going to have to teach my future husband how to fuck me or just resort to a sex toy drawer to fulfill my fantasies." Going after the kind of guy I want is dangerous—I've seen how that works out.

"Maksim is smitten with you. I see the way he looks at you. There's no way that man isn't going to toss you around in the bedroom."

She's right. I know she is. Sometimes I hate myself for only seeing myself as a plain Jane, but I look identical to my mother. The dimple. The curls. The sweet demeanor as though she'd harm no one. My dad's mistress was blonde, with dark eyeliner and red lipstick. She wore short dresses that clung to her ass and breasts with high heels that made her legs go on for miles. Eventually, men tire of the girl next door. She seems like a good idea when you're looking for someone to mother your children, but that gets old fast.

The night my dad left, I swore I'd never allow myself to get in a relationship like that. His absence set off a phase in high school, one I'm not proud of, where I was the girl who'd fool around with anyone. Of course, I kept it to the public school boys. Boys who lived in my neighborhood and didn't attend the private school I went to. They thought I was that much more appealing because of the Catholic schoolgirl uniform—"Wear your short plaid skirt," they'd say.

I shake my head, wanting to forget that girl. It's the one piece of my life I've never shared with Jana.

"Want to bet it's Italian?" I say.

"My money's on Maksim being more original than that, but wear a dark color just in case the sauce splashes up on you."

"I'm just going to wear my boring black dress then." I get up off the bed and take it off the hanger.

"I hope he surprises you."

"Me too."

"I'll be crossing my fingers for some doggie style in your future." She laughs, and we both say goodbye before hanging up.

I stare at the black dress I wear on almost every date. It's simple, and I can pair it with a jean jacket and sandals to tone it down, depending on what he's wearing when he shows up. I make my hair a little bouncier, spray the curls in place. My makeup is light, barely there, a natural look with my lips a little pinker than normal.

The doorbell rings a minute later, and I take one last look at myself, preparing the standard date answers as to why I chose psychology, where I went to school, how long it will be until my practice is doing well. I open the door and find Maksim in shorts, a T-shirt, and a sweatshirt over top, looking handsome as ever and casual.

"Um." I look down at myself. Even if I put on my jacket and sandals, I'm still way over dressed.

"Yeah, go change into shorts and a T-shirt while I snoop." He walks into my house without an invite.

There's a comeback on the tip of my tongue, but I kind of like his take-charge behavior.

"There's nothing to find." I smile, leaving him in my small living room while I head to the bathroom.

"We'll see about that. Hurry up, I've got reservations."

"Where?"

"You'll see."

---

*S*itting in Maksim's Mercedes, one that almost looks as if it's matchbook-sized compared to him, the scent of his aftershave or his cologne makes my body hum. Now that I'm here with him and we're really doing this, my nerves are working overtime. I was prepared to sleep with Maksim when we were in Toronto, but I have a feeling that being wooed by Maksim will be something else entirely.

"Where are we going?" I ask.

He smiles at me as he heads onto the freeway. "It's a surprise. Sorry to disappoint you if you thought I was going to take you to a fancy restaurant."

"No. I'm not disappointed." I'm not, although I did assume.

"You thought that, didn't you?" He grins, and the way it lights up his crystal-blue eyes should be criminal.

I shake my head, but my smile gives me away and his grin widens. "Maybe."

"I'm more original than that." He winks.

Isn't that the problem though? He's unlike any other man I've ever met, and the harder I try to push aside any curiosity I have for this man, the more he pulls me in.

"I guess we'll see."

"Are you challenging me?"

"Maybe." I shrug.

"How many dates do you think I can plan before I do something unoriginal like dinner and a movie?"

I shift in my seat to face him, curious where this line of conversation is going. I'd love to go on more dates with this man, especially since the bubbly feeling in my stomach is a nice change of pace. But I don't want to get my hopes up. "Who's the one to decide unoriginal versus original?"

"I think we can manage that ourselves. How many?"

"Two," I say.

He groans. "*Kotik*, you're making this too easy."

I chuckle. "Okay." I don't want to make it too hard for him. I'm not sure how many dates I could plan that were original. "Five."

"Let's say nine. It is my lucky number." He looks away from the highway for a moment and grins at me.

"Nine dates?" My eyes are wide as he nods. "You're going to commit to nine dates with me?"

When he pulls off the highway, the car idles at a stoplight and he glances at me, his eyes holding a devilish glint. "I'd commit to an infinite amount of dates with you."

I'd like to say "only until you find someone else who interests you more," but I push that thought aside, excited to see him even attempt nine.

"And what do you get if you pull off nine original dates?" I ask.

"If I succeed, then you have to plan an unoriginal date for me."

I nod in agreement. "And if you lose?"

"We can do an honest therapy session and I won't come on to you once."

How can I turn that down? I hold out my hand. "Deal."

He takes it, and heat courses through my veins from where our skin meets. "Free up your calendar, Miss Paisley."

"That's Dr. Paisley."

"Now you're putting thoughts in my head of you in a white coat and naked underneath. I think I want to change up my reward after the nine dates." His hands tighten on the steering wheel and he turns onto the main road.

"What do you have in mind?" It's hard to hold back my smile.

"A little doctor/patient role-playing?"

I smile and bite my lip. "That can be arranged."

He squirms in his seat. "Damn, you've got me tense now."

I laugh and he does too. We continue to drive, butterflies filling my stomach at the possibility of what this could be. What could grow between us. I don't want to be hopeful, but the trouble with number nine is that he makes it so hard not to be.

He pulls into our destination and I'm shocked. Never in my life has anyone ever taken me to an amusement park.

"Busch Gardens?" I ask.

"You do ride roller coasters?" He follows the attendant's directions and parks his Mercedes.

"I do." That's not really true. I hate rollercoasters but I don't want to put a damper on this date when he went to the effort of planning it.

"Great. And they have pretzels here. Maybe I'll finally get that answer on why you pick pretzels over nachos." He turns off the engine, folds himself out of his Mercedes, and meets me at the hood of his car.

People look on, mostly families leaving the park with kids passed out in their parents' arms. Maksim takes my hand and escorts me over to the tram to take us into the park as though he's just an average guy. He's so far from average it's not even funny.

As we wait for the tram, I can't help but notice how small my hand feels in his large one. I look up at him—the stubble along his jaw, the slightly crooked nose, his strong jawline that I can't wait to lick. The natural blond highlights in his hair that I'm dying to run my hands through.

"Keep looking at me like that and we're not gonna make it on the tram, *kotik*."

"Promise?" I grin cheekily at him.

He looks down at me and his tongue slides out along his bottom lip. "Tell me one thing…"

"What?" I'm already breathless.

"Do you kiss after the first date?" I open my mouth to respond, but he holds up a finger. "Hold that thought."

The tram arrives and we file into the back row. There are fewer people going in at this time of day.

Something occurs to me while we sit there and wait for everyone to get situated. I don't want to be the shy girl who waits for a kiss. Not at all. Something about this man makes me not want to play it safe.

"So, do you kiss after the first date?" Maksim asks again once the tram moves.

I turn toward him, my hand sliding into the hair at the back of his head. "I kiss *on* the first date."

My lips touch his and he wastes no time sliding his tongue into my mouth. Our kiss only lasts seconds, but I'll never forget that feeling, as though I'm lifting off in a hot air balloon when his lips meet mine.

"We have to be semi-careful because we're in public," he whispers. "Wouldn't want my doctor to lose her license for sleeping with the patient." His breath tickles my ear, and he places the softest kiss right under my earlobe.

I realize suddenly that this is probably part of the reason we're here, so far from where we live. He doesn't want us to accidentally run into someone from the team.

I'm completely screwed. All I want to do is straddle him and beg him to fuck me right here, damn my license. But I sit nicely, trying to remember the last time I was at Busch Gardens and where all the hiding places are so we can have some make-out time.

He pays for my ticket, and we walk into the park. He pulls a ball cap from his back pocket, though it doesn't do the best job of hiding who he is. I still see the fingers pointed in his direction and the hushed whispers, but no one comes right up to us.

"Shall we?" He looks at the biggest and scariest roller coaster at the park.

My stomach rumbles. I lied when I told him I was into roller coasters, but I don't want to be that girl, so I buck up and say, "Definitely."

Twenty minutes later, the harness comes down over my shoulders and I fear I might die of a heart attack with the way my heart is practically beating out of my chest. Maybe the headline could read, "Sweet girl dies trying to be someone she's not."

CHAPTER 13

"Impressive, Petrov."

Maksim

The most thrilling part of riding a roller coaster is when the cart tips over the top of the hill. The most anticipation comes with the slow climb up the first hill. On the way up, I glance at Paisley—she's pale and gripping the harness so tightly, it might take a crowbar for her to release it.

"Are you positive you like roller coasters?" I ask.

She says nothing but nods enthusiastically.

"You don't look excited."

We're approaching the top of the hill and I catch her closing her eyes. "I am. Just this hill… and I haven't ridden one in a while."

Blin. I picked the wrong date.

I watch her, not believing her act. The park is strewn out below us and the cart starts to tip forward as we crest the hill. A painful sound erupts out of her, then she screams. A loud, piercing scream that makes me close my own eyes. We're down one hill and already climbing another.

"Okay, I lied. I hate roller coasters…" Her screams make it sound as if someone is chasing her with a knife. "Holy shit!"

I leave all the questions that want to rush out of my

mouth for later. Why did she tell me she likes roller coasters if she doesn't?

By the time the ride ends, her curly hair is windblown. A relieved breath falls out of her when the harness unclips and raises over our heads.

"Thank God," she says, stepping out.

Paisley walks so fast down the exit ramp, I can barely keep pace and I'm practically double her size. A kid stops me for an autograph, then I finally catch up to her at the end of the exit ramp. She's on a bench, bent over and catching her breath. I sit down next to her, stretching my arm out along the back of the bench.

She looks at me from the corner of her eye. "I'm sorry."

"You have nothing to be sorry for. Are you okay?" I rub her back. I don't care that she lied about liking roller coasters. If anything, it's awesome that she tried to suck it up since I brought us here for our date. She was trying to make the most of it, a quality I admire.

"I'm good now." She sits up straight.

"You didn't have to lie just because I brought you here. I never want you to do something you're not comfortable with just for my sake."

She swivels my way. "I didn't want to seem like I don't know how to have fun. I didn't want to be a buzzkill and tell you I hate roller coasters."

I slide closer to her. "You never have to pretend to be anything but who you are."

She chews on the inside of her cheek and stares at me for a moment. "I'm not really a 'live life on the edge' kind of woman."

I smile. "I know."

"You're going to find out I'm kind of boring."

God, she's so fucking adorable. "There's nothing boring about you."

"You barely know me."

"I don't make a habit of falling for boring women, *kotik*. That's why I like your claws." I link my hand with hers and pull her up off the park bench. "Time for us to go on a train ride."

We walk through the entrance of the Serengeti Express Train, and I select the back row so no one has a chance to interrupt us. The good thing about coming to the park at this hour is that most families have gone home and the guests here are only interested in the roller coasters and not a boring train ride. The train moves and my thumb runs along her forefinger.

"I'd never have asked you out if I wasn't interested in you. I want to get to know the real Paisley Pearce, not the Paisley Pearce you think I want you to be." She stares at the horizon, and I place my finger on her chin to bring her face to mine. "Agreed?"

Her soft brown eyes are so beautiful I could lose myself in them. "Okay."

"That's it? That was easy. You're just going to agree? Doesn't seem like the Paisley Pearce I've gotten to know so far."

She shrugs and gives me a small smile. "I want to be different. I want to love roller coasters and be that girl who's secure enough with herself to wear a short dress to a club and dance on a table."

"Whoa now. Maybe I haven't mentioned how possessive I can be."

She laughs, and her curls bounce when she tilts her head. "I've always just been the conservative girl."

"Maybe that's what I'm into?" I wrap my arm around her shoulders and pull her toward me.

"No one likes the conservative girl. They like the fun girl."

I kiss the top of her head. "How about this? You try some things you wouldn't ordinarily do with me, but you tell me because I only care about knowing the real you. Then we'll do whatever it is together."

She tilts her head and looks up at me. I love how everything feels so natural with her. As if we've been together forever.

"Thanks," she says.

I know we're not anywhere near the end of this issue with her, but I have to get her to understand that she's the one I want, and I don't find her the least bit boring.

She raises her arm and her hand wraps around the back of my neck. She leans in until our lips meet.

Damn, she can kiss. I slip my tongue into her mouth, and her moan is enough to make me want to pull her off this train and lay her down on the field we're rolling past. We keep the kiss short, and I miss her lips the minute they're off mine.

"Can we ride another roller coaster?" she whispers.

I chuckle. "Why?"

"Because I want to try it again. Now that I can tell you I'm terrified, I think you might help me through it."

My eyes lock with hers. "Okay, but you tell me when you've had enough."

"Deal." She smiles and kisses me on the cheek.

After the train ride ends, we file out and get in line for another roller coaster. Paisley's patient and understanding when it comes to me being recognized. She volunteers to take pictures of me with the fans and even pulls a pen out of her purse when a kid comes up and his dad doesn't have anything to write with.

We ride three more roller coasters, and she screams so

hard I fear she'll have lung damage. After that, we decide to grab some pizza.

"All right, tell me why pretzel over nachos?"

"Why are you so curious about that?" She bites into her slice. Her hair is pulled back in a ponytail now, the last roller coaster having destroyed her curls, according to her. But there's one strand she missed on the side, and I can't stop staring at it.

"Because they both have cheese, but one is crispy and one is soft. I think why you chose pretzels might say a lot about you."

She nods. "Maybe you should've gone into psychology."

We both laugh.

"You're dodging the question." I point my piece of pizza at her.

"I find the pretzel comforting, but I do like nachos. I just like nachos that are overfilled with meat, cheese, sour cream, guacamole. All the good stuff. It's hard to handle that in an arena seat."

"I'll have to remember that."

"Which do you prefer?" she asks.

"I would've gotten a hamburger or hot dog. I prefer protein." I wink.

She giggles, falling back on her stool. "I think that's supposed to be my line."

"It would be if we were talking about my meat."

She laughs harder, and if we weren't surrounded by so many people, I'd stand up, lean over this table, and kiss the living shit out of her because she's so damn cute when she's having fun.

After we finish our pizza, we end up walking through the area filled with carnival games. Every vendor screams at us to try to win a prize.

"Want me to win you a stuffed animal?" I ask her.

"Are you that confident you can win one? You know these games are fixed."

I lead her toward some of the games, ignoring her judgment of my skills. Isn't this what happens when you go to an amusement park? Her arms should be filled with prizes when we leave.

We end up at the basketball hoop, and I miss all three times.

Paisley says nothing to make me feel bad about it, but tension creeps into my chest.

Then we go over to the game where you have to throw a dart at a balloon. I pop one balloon, but that's all. We walk away empty-handed—again.

"Let's just go on another ride. We could do a water ride?" Paisley suggests.

There's not a chance we're leaving here until I win her something. "No, let's do this bottle cap one."

I lead her over to where I have to get a ring over a bottle cap. Paisley tries too and she gets more than I do, but neither of us win.

"One of these games is mine," I say.

She winds her arm through mine. "I don't need a cheap stuffed animal, Maksim. Let's go enjoy the rest of our night."

She's crazy if she thinks I'm going to give up on this. One thing she needs to know about me—I'm a professional athlete and therefore competitive as hell. "No. There's got to be one here that I can win."

Stopping at the rubber ducks, Paisley hands money to the woman and looks at me. "Pick one."

I give her a small glare that she has such little faith in me. This game is just luck, no skill involved.

"We're wasting money doing all the games we can't win," she says.

I shrug. "I have the money to blow."

She leans back and her eyes go wide. "Well, Mr. Moneybags, excuse me. Now, pick a duck."

I grab a duck, hoping I've picked the one that will win the best prize. Unfortunately, I win a rubber duck. As in one that's exactly like the one they're using for the game.

"Way to go." The woman working the game pats my hand as I accept the prize.

Paisley holds up the rubber duck in front of her. "What should we name her?"

"Who said it's a her?" I ask.

"Impressive, Petrov. You sure know how to pick your ducks." She hip checks me.

I can't help but smile even though I feel like a loser who couldn't actually win her anything.

"Yeah," I say with a lack of enthusiasm. "Should we give it to some kid?"

Her brows furrow and her expression questions my audacity. "This is my prize. She's mine to always remember tonight."

"All I had to do was pick a duck," I grumble.

She pulls me over to a more secluded area. "I should thank you properly."

"What does that mean?"

She pushes me so my back hits the concrete wall and steps closer to me. Rising on her tiptoes, she gives me another kiss that speeds up my pulse and makes my dick twitch.

Afterward we walk for a while. But I figure we should probably head home since we have a long drive ahead of us.

"One more ride, you choose," she says.

I lead her to the closest one because I'm ready to have her completely to myself. We leave the rubber duck—who is yet to have a name—with the attendant. I warn him if anything happens to the thing, we're going to have words, and he looks at me like I'm crazy because, yeah, it's just a rubber duck. But it seems to mean something to Paisley which means it means something to me.

"Cart one?" I ask Paisley, knowing this could be her breaking point.

"Okay."

The roller coaster isn't as big as the others, so she should be fine. "I'll hold your hand the entire time."

"Deal." We climb in the first cart, and I take her hand.

We roll slowly up the hill. From the rides earlier this evening, I know that she hates the first hill, so I let her squeeze me as much as possible.

"You got this," I say to her.

She nods, then the roller coaster peaks over the first hill. Our cart teeters there, looking down over what's below us—concrete and metal.

The roller coaster halts and we don't move at all.

"Oh, man, it broke," a guy behind us says.

"You good?" I ask Paisley, looking over to see her eyes squeezed shut.

"Maksim?" she whispers.

"Yeah?"

"I think I've had enough."

I bite down my laugh and squeeze her hand again. "Deal."

Chapter 14

Paisley

Thus far, Maksim has made good on planning original dates. Today he took me to a donut place before we had to be at the arena to meet with the at-risk youth. We've done no more than kiss, and he doesn't seem as eager as I am for more. After the amusement park, he dropped me off at my house, kissed me goodbye, and I watched him walk down the pathway back to his car.

"Next week you're coming with us to Nashville, right?" he asks me, caging me into a dark corner in the back hallway of the arena.

"I am, and speaking of the team, I need to report a meeting with you to Mr. Gerhardt."

"All in due time. Back to Nashville—plan on one of our dates while we're there." He kisses the delicate flesh under my earlobe.

"We can't have a date when I'm with the team."

How on earth does he think that would work? We might as well announce we're dating to everyone. I know I'm not really treating Maksim, so technically it's a bit of a gray area, but no one else knows that.

"Trust me. We'll be fine."

"Maksim."

He places his finger to my lips. "Trust me."

This man is making me forget my better judgment. I nod and he bends down again, this time replacing his finger with his lips. I slip my tongue through his parted lips, and a strangled groan rushes up his throat. His hands tighten on my hips and he breaches any distance between us, rubbing his huge hard-on against my stomach. We both lose control and forget where we are, our tongues battling for supremacy, our hands clenching on the other, pulling, tugging, and grinding.

He closes the kiss and rests his forehead against mine, breathing heavily as his fingers grip my hips. "I'm not sure how much longer I'm going to make it."

"No one put a stipulation on how many dates until we sleep together." My insides contract with my words. I'm desperate to have this man in my bed.

"I did. It's kissing only until all nine dates are complete. I want you to know what kind of guy I am. That I'm not who you think."

My fingers thread through his hair. I love the blond strands against his darker roots. "You have nothing to prove. I never should've assumed. I already know what kind of man you are."

His head rocks side to side as his forehead stays glued to mine. "No. I want to do this even with the blue balls it's giving me. You mean a lot to me, and when the time comes, I want you to be as sure as you are the sky is blue."

My thighs clench. It's only been two dates, which means I have seven more to go. "How fast can you make these dates happen?"

He laughs, and I love the deep timbre of his chuckle. It vibrates down to the pit of my stomach and warms there like brandy. "It won't take too long."

And then with one quick kiss, he's backing away from me.

We fall in line again as though we're just two acquaintances heading down the hall. The sounds of footsteps from our little Fury Juniors coming down the hallway fills the space.

"Hey, I forgot to talk to you," Maksim says. "Do you mind if I just work with Dru and Malcolm today? You could maybe give a tour of the arena to the others. They're embarrassed—"

This time I look both ways and place my finger to his lips. "No problem."

He smiles and opens his mouth, his tongue sliding around my finger. I knew he had a magical tongue, but holy shit, I want to fall to my back and spread my legs and let him use those masterful skills between my thighs. He kisses the tip of my finger, and I'm pretty sure my mouth could inhale a swarm of flies it's open so wide.

"Thanks," he says.

Just before the group is far enough down the hall where they can see us, he walks away, leaving me speechless.

For the first half hour of our time together, I take the rest of the group on a tour. We visit the offices and press boxes, then walk through the empty arena, past all the concession stands that would normally be lined up with people. Then we head back down and I show them the press room where the players do interviews after the games, and finally the locker room where each spot has a jersey hanging up for each player.

"They all shower together?" Lark asks. "Weird."

"They're all men," I say.

"Still. They make so much money and they all have to see one another naked?" Lark's look of disgust makes me look at Jana, who showed up a few minutes into the tour.

"Want to see one of the suites?" Jana asks.

A unanimous yes sounds from the group, so Jana takes

us to an elevator. Using her key to the Gerhardts' suite, she opens the door and allows everyone to file in.

"Man, talk about money," one of the boys says, going to where the inside meets the outside. "Hey, there's Malcolm."

Oh shit, I completely forgot.

"Hey, everyone, let's head back to the concession area. Maybe we can make a big pretzel. You have to be hungry." I urgently weave through them to block any view of the boys and Maksim, but my feet come to a stop when I see what's happening.

"He's really good," Marin says, a hint of adoration in her tone.

Malcolm has a stick and he's moving the puck around the ice. Dru is continuing to skate the oval and doing pretty damn well. Maksim comes up behind Malcolm and puts his hands over Malcolm's to show him how to handle the puck.

"I want to learn too," Lark says.

"Okay, let's go then." I can't take my eyes off of Maksim.

Dru falls and Maksim flawlessly helps him up and looks like he gestures for Dru to keep going. Malcolm skates toward the goal and gets the puck in the net, the light on top flashing. He grows so excited he lifts his arms, only to lose his footing and fall on his ass.

"He scored!" Marin exclaims.

Maksim screams a huge WOO-HOO that echoes through the arena and Malcolm smiles a big toothy smile as my heart leaps.

I don't need nine dates to know how special this man is.

"*Y*ou owe me for this," Jana says from the other end of the phone.

"I'm sorry, but I don't feel comfortable going on this date." I apologize for the umpteenth time since Mr. Gerhardt called and told me he'd set up a date for me.

That's how he does things. He doesn't ask permission, just does whatever he thinks is best, and to him, I'm his daughter's lonely friend who needs a social life. Never mind that I'm seven dates away from sleeping with a member of his team.

"I thought you and Maksim aren't exclusive?" Jana asks.

"Well, I'm not asking him if we are." I've never felt so in limbo with someone. I think we're only seeing one another, but I don't have the nerve to outright ask. "All I know is *I'm* not comfortable going out with someone else."

"You do know it's some guy from my dad's country club. Like the tournament planner or something. I have nothing to wear that fits what he'll be looking for."

"Jana, you're gorgeous. I'm sure whatever you wear he's going to love."

"You better nail Maksim, and I want all the details after you do. That's payback for making me go on a date with this guy. And you need to tell my dad to stop fixing you up."

I open my bag of sour cream and onion chips, pop one in my mouth, and eat it.

"Are you eating? You'd better be going out with him tonight." There's anger in her tone because Jana hates blind dates. One time she showed up and the guy made her pay the bill in full since she was Jana Gerhardt and the entire conversation was filled with questions about her trust fund.

"You know they have that bachelor party for that trainer on the team."

She groans. "You should've gone on the date. He's going to be at strip clubs and you're sitting at home in your pajamas, eating what sounds like potato chips and probably watching Netflix by yourself."

"Come over after the date."

"I'm going to call and cancel," she says.

"No! I don't want your dad to know I didn't go. If you show up and make an excuse for me, he'll be pleasantly surprised. If we just cancel, he'll call your dad and your dad will call me, then I'm either going to have to lie outright or crumble and tell the truth."

She laughs. "Man, Paise, I love you, but you think too hard on things. Just tell my dad you don't want to be fixed up."

I should take her advice, but Mr. Gerhardt has been sort of like the father I never had—at least since my parents divorced and my dad started his new life. He worries about me and my well-being. I don't want to disappoint him.

"Just come over after the date. I'll call you and you can say something came up."

She groans. "I hate doing that. They always know it's fake. Then they think I'm stuck up…" I let her ramble on while I get comfortable on my couch and scan Netflix for a show to binge this weekend. "You know what I mean?"

"Yep," I say, not really knowing what she said.

"Keep your phone on you in case I send a 911 text!" Her voice rises.

"I will."

She groans again. "Okay bye."

"Chin up. Maybe he's gorgeous and a great guy."

"Doubtful." She hangs up.

I place my phone down on the coffee table. Just the thought of Maksim sitting in some velvet chair with a half-naked woman in front of him, shaking her ass and her tits splayed in front of his face, makes my appetite disappear. Jana's right. While he's sliding dollar bills in a G-string, I should be out having my own fun. I need to be prepared for when this thing goes south.

I've been trying to tamp down any expectations I have for Maksim, but it's harder every time I see him. He's so attentive and sweet and really seems to like me for me. But once we part for the night, that nagging in the back of my head returns, reminding me that my mom won over my dad once upon a time too. And after she popped out a kid and he took a back seat to motherhood, he hightailed it out of town with a newer, shinier model.

Sometimes I think the therapy I did in college while earning my degree wasn't enough. I should be going to see someone now that I'm grown and need to find a healthy relationship.

The honk of a horn outside sounds, and I roll my eyes that one of my neighbors has plans. I'm used to spending my nights like this, so why should tonight feel any different? Because lately I've been spending time with Maksim, and when I'm not, Jana finds her way over.

The horn honks again. This time longer.

I push the blanket off my lap and look outside to see Maksim's Mercedes parked outside. What the hell is he doing?

I look down at myself in my pajamas. Shit. Picking up my phone, I dial his number.

The minute the call connects, Maksim doesn't answer

with a hello, but rather, "Get your sweet ass down here, I'm taking you on date number three."

"Um, I have to change."

"No changing. Don't worry, no one will see you. We're going somewhere private."

"I'm in pajamas," I say in a low voice.

"All the better. Come on, I'll put the seat warmer on for you."

Although we're in Florida and it's somewhat warm this time of year, I'm in a tank top with no bra and a pair of pajama shorts that I'm fairly sure show off half my ass. But I guess if I want to tempt him to cross that line sooner than the nine dates, this isn't a bad outfit to do it in.

I grab my keys, my purse, and leave my apartment.

I wasn't prepared for the smoldering look from Maksim though. The minute I sit in the passenger seat of his Mercedes, the energy shifts. Maybe I bargained for more than I was ready for.

CHAPTER 15

Maksim

"Yeah, I was wrong. Go change." I keep my eyes facing the windshield, hands gripping the steering wheel tightly.

There's no way I'm going to continue our date with her in that outfit.

"I told you I was in my pajamas," she says, not reaching for the door.

"I thought you'd be wearing something with more fabric." My fingers tighten on the leather steering wheel even more and my hands ache.

"Hmm… I'm thinking I should refuse. Tempt you." She leans back in the seat.

I peek over and see her nipples erect through the tight tank top. "I swear, Paisley, if you don't leave this car and go change, I cannot be responsible for what I do."

Her legs widen. "Maybe I want you to go all caveman on me."

Fuck. Is this another one of her acts or is this her? As much as I'd like to think she's just fucking with me, I'm pretty sure she's not. As my pants get snugger, I mentally repeat to myself that if I break now, she might always think that's why I'm with her.

"Go change, Paisley," I bite out. "Please."

Her hand reaches for the car door. Thank fuck.

"Since you asked so nicely." The passenger door opens and she's got one foot out of the door when she turns in my direction. "Feel free to watch me walking away."

And watch I do, with my fist in my mouth so I don't scream for her to return and straddle me in the front seat.

She walks back to my car five minutes later in a pair of sweatpants and a T-shirt with a bra underneath. What was I thinking in telling her to change? The only piece of skin showing now is a strip along her stomach.

"Better?"

"Better so I don't go animalistic on you, yes." I start the engine and pull away from the curb.

"You're aware that it's you keeping us from moving forward to the next stage of our relationship?"

"I'm fully aware."

She giggles and scoots in her seat to get comfortable. "I love your car."

I run my hand down the steering wheel. "Thanks. You look good in it."

A blush rushes up her neck. I so badly want to see that travel the length of her body.

We arrive at the candy store ten minutes later.

"You've taken me to a closed strip mall? Definitely original."

I turn off the ignition and open up my door. "Just wait and see." Rounding the front of my car, I open the passenger door and hold out my hand.

"Just so you know I scream really loud." She accepts my hand, and I pull her out of the car and into my arms, wrapping an arm around her waist.

"That was made clear on the roller coaster, *kotik*." I kiss her forehead, the smell of lavender and vanilla floating up to my nostrils.

She tilts her head up to look at me.

"Hello," I say.

"Hi," she says and I kiss her briefly. "I hope that means you're not going to kill me."

I drag her toward the candy store. "Believe me, I'm not killing you until I have all of you."

"Oh, well, that's refreshing."

I chuckle at her sense of humor. Ever since the amusement park, I've tried to figure out why she felt she needed to be someone she wasn't with me. I'm attracted to her for her intelligence, her wry humor, her kindness. Why does she feel that's not enough to fulfill my needs?

Nolan, Roadie's teenage son, comes out of the store when he sees us approaching. I hand him a fifty and he pockets it. "I'll be in my car to lock up when you're done."

"Thanks, Nolan."

He nods and holds the door open for Paisley to walk in, waggling his eyebrows. I shove him in the chest and hear his laughter until the door shuts.

"So you're going to kill me with sugar?" Paisley asks, perusing the rows of different candy in plastic bins.

"The store is yours. Whatever you want."

She turns, and the dim light catches her smile. "Anything I want? Hmm…"

"Even the chocolate," I say.

"Ohh… you spoil me, Maksim Petrov."

I walk to her and swing one arm around her waist, pulling her back to my chest. How am I ever going to go through the agony of six more dates before I'm inside her? "Have you ever had a guy sneak you into a candy shop after hours?"

She giggles and I slide her hair off her shoulder with my free hand. "Nope, this is original."

"Definitely original." I kiss her neck and slap her ass. "Now go pick out some candy."

She scoots forward, almost running away from me.

"Let's see what we can tell about one another from the candy we pick out?" She opens up a case of gummy something and steals one.

"The fact that you ate the gummy bear's head off, I'm thinking I need to take back the rights to our little rubber ducky."

She laughs and her head falls back, making her curls bounce. I love making her laugh. She throws the rest of the gummy bear in the air and catches it in her mouth, chewing it dramatically. "We do need to name our duck."

"Our duck, huh?" I like how that sounds coming out of her mouth.

"I'll gladly take on full custody rights if you'd like to abandon her." She takes a handful of sour balls and brings one after the other into her mouth.

"I'm not abandoning her."

"You haven't come to visit her. I had her in the bath with me the other night and we both missed you." She pretends to whine.

That brings to mind a visual that's better saved for when we're not in a public place. I clear my throat and then look away from her. "I'm heading over to the chocolate."

She laughs, probably knowing the effect she has on me.

Leaving her, I go over to the chocolate bins, pick up a bag, and fill it.

"I give you props, three original ideas on dates," she says from across the room. "This isn't from too much practice, is it?"

I look up from the chocolate-covered almonds. "Are you suggesting I'm a serial dater and take different women to all the same original places?"

She shrugs, the easy expression from earlier gone from her face. "What can I say? I have some issues."

I abandon my bag and grab a bag for her. "Fill up your bag, then we're heading out to the beach. You're going to tell me who hurt you."

She accepts the bag but doesn't move. "You want me to open up all this baggage I'm carrying and show you what's inside?"

I make sure she's looking into my eyes so that she can see my sincerity when I say, "I want to know everything about you."

She gives me a small smile and turns and fills her bag. Hopefully she's ready to open up to me.

Ten minutes and two bags of candy later, Nolan meets us at the door. I hand him a hundred-dollar bill that more than pays for the candy, and we head back to my Mercedes.

"The beach, huh? Is that considered date four or are we still on date three?" she asks.

I think for a moment. How can I make a walk on the beach unique in some way? "Maybe if we go shark diving?"

She laughs and her brows crinkle. "I don't ride roller coasters. What makes you think I'd go shark diving?"

"True. FYI, I'm not cool with that either."

"Really?" She seems surprised.

"Do you think of me as less than a man?" I could add that sharks and pretty much any mammal that lives in the water scare the crap out of me, but I don't.

"Your man card is intact with the fact that you're a professional hockey player."

I run my hand over my forehead. "Phew."

We drive toward the beach. A sign on the side of the road gives me an idea of how to squeeze two dates into one.

"I have to make a quick stop." I pull over at a convenience store, run in, and buy what I need.

When I get back in the car, I hold up the box of garbage bags.

She doesn't smile or laugh, but inches closer to the door. "You're going to take me to a beach late at night and you bought black trash bags?"

It takes me a second to clue in to where she's coming from, but when I do, I can't stop laughing.

"Maks?"

Something about her shortening my name feels like a tug on my chest. "I thought we could pick up trash. You know, instead of adopt a road, adopt a beach. As much as we need to in order for this to be considered our fourth date."

"Hmm. How about this… I've never had anyone feed me candy while I walked on the beach."

I toss the trash bags in the back seat. "Much better idea."

She places her hand on my thigh. "Not that I would mind picking up trash one day, but I'd like some gloves."

Man, I feel like such an idiot for my suggestion, but I'm working on the fly here. Then again, her hand is on my thigh and she's running it up and down, so it seems to have worked out. Score.

We arrive at the beach and bring our bags of candy with us. We stand side by side in the sand, staring at the dark water. The moon is full and reflects off the water, and in the sky are tall clouds miles and miles off into the Gulf. They light up with a flash of lightning inside them every once in a while. There's not much of a breeze, so the waves gently lap at the shore.

"There's something about the darkness of the Gulf at night," she says. "It doesn't make it as magical. It makes me think there's some dark stuff going on in that water."

"I've never really thought about it. The darkness is kind of eerie though. But don't worry, I'm here to protect you."

"Unless you plan on throwing me in the water, I think I'm safe." She opens her bag of candy. "Gummy bear, please."

I pick out a gummy bear and place it on her tongue. "The start of our fourth date."

I hold out my bag and she picks a malted chocolate ball, putting it in my mouth. We walk for a while.

I wait for her to bring up whoever this guy is who's causing me problems now, but she only makes small talk and asks me to feed her candy. Guess I'm going to have to push the issue. It's now or never.

"Who's the guy that I'm gonna prove is a dickhead?" I ask.

She blows out a breath and stops walking, looking out at the water. "No judging?"

"Never." I sit down on the sand and wait for her to join me.

She does and takes a peanut butter cup and shoves it in my mouth. "My dad."

My eyebrows raise.

"He left my mom when I was in middle school. Married another woman."

"Oh." Not at all what I expected.

"It's complicated. The woman he left my mom for was the complete opposite of her. I'm just like my mom."

"So your mom is gorgeous and intelligent?"

She smiles at me. "You are a sweet talker, Petrov, and yes, she is. But she's also the girl next door. The organizer. The planner. The type A personality."

"All admirable traits." I'm not sure I understand what the problem is.

"She's not the fun one, Maksim, and neither am I. I'm not the crazy 'dance and drink all night' woman. I'm not the kind of woman a man loses himself in. The woman who always keeps him on his toes. I'm a 'make sure all the bills are paid' girl, my calendar is fully color coded."

"This is what you're worried about? That I'll think you're boring?"

"Yes. Maybe not now, but eventually."

"Open up." I shove a handful of sour balls in her mouth. "My turn now."

"Mmm…" she says, but I shake my head.

"Did you ever stop to think that maybe those are things I want in a partner? Or that your dad is just some asshole who didn't know how lucky he was? I love the fact you wouldn't let me out of the therapy. That you had to check that box in your head. The approved snack list you gave the Fury Juniors? Genius. And let's remember you rode roller coasters with me, and I bet if I did want to go shark diving, you'd agree eventually. You might be terrified, but you'd trust me to keep you safe. And do you know how fucking sexy it is that you have no idea that ten different guys check you out every time you enter a room? You're blind to how my entire world has been turned upside down since you stepped into it. I wish you could see yourself the way I do. You're so much more than you give yourself credit for. Paisley, you're everything and more to me, exactly how you are."

She swallows and looks at me for a moment. Just when

she looks as if she's going to speak, she tackles me to the sand and kisses me as though I'm the last man on earth.

I guess I said the right thing.

CHAPTER 16

"You've put a fucking spell on me."

Paisley

I lose control of myself. Screw his rule of nine dates. This man has won me over with his words and the feeling behind them.

I straddle him on the sand, press my lips to his, and kiss him as though the world is about to end. His strong hands grab my hips and I grind along his increasingly hard length, needing to quench the flame that's been burning on high between us for weeks. Screw the fact he's technically my client—at least to all the world—and we shouldn't be together.

I tear my lips off his and sprinkle his face with kisses. "You're an amazing guy."

He chuckles, and his fingertips move up over the waistband of my sweats and onto my bare midriff. "Hold on, we still have five more dates."

I sit up and press my hands to his chest. He's wearing a button-down shirt and slacks since he was at the bachelor party. I totally forgot to ask why he ditched that to be with me.

"I'm relinquishing that deal. You can still take me on the dates, but we're done with the just kissing thing."

I circle my hips over his middle and a pained expression crosses his face. "But I had plans," he groans.

I unbutton the bottom button of his shirt, revealing his treasure trail. He doesn't fight me, so I continue to undress him. "So do I."

"I think I'm going to lose this battle."

I nod. "I guarantee you're about to lose it."

Once his shirt is unbuttoned, I splay my hands on his hard chest and push the material aside, showcasing his amazing, toned stomach with ripped abs. "Jeez, do you ever work out?"

"Not impressed?" he asks with a cocky grin because he knows there's no possible way I couldn't be.

"Maybe a few more hours at the gym wouldn't hurt."

He grabs my hips, flips me onto my back in the sand, and uses his knees to open my legs for him to slide between. "Cardio might help. Want to be my partner?"

I wind my arms around his neck and my fingers play with the hair at the back of his head. "I'm nothing if not helpful."

He laughs and his lips fall to mine, searing me with a kiss. Then before I can protest, he's up, standing over me and holding out his hand for me to take. "Not here. We'll have sex on the beach at some point, but not our first time."

I take his hand and he pulls me up, kissing me once more like he can't stop himself. No complaints here. He scoops me up, so I straddle him, his hands going to my ass.

"The candy," I say right before we walk away.

He laughs. "Seriously?"

"You'll be thanking me once we're naked and spent in bed in an hour."

Bending over and lowering us, Maksim shows how strong he is. I snatch up the two bags of candy and he rises back up to full height. "I hate to break it to you, *kotik*, but you'll be lucky if you're eating that candy at all in the next twelve hours."

I laugh, my forehead falling to his shoulder. "Aren't we arrogant."

"Talk to me after we're done and let me know if you think my arrogance is undeserved."

"Okay, Rico Suave."

He smacks my ass while keeping me glued to him as he makes his way down the beach to the car. My core tingles with anticipation at the way he manhandles me. I can only pray this continues when we get into a bedroom.

We arrive at my apartment since it's closest. Maksim's hands have barely left my body since we climbed out of his car. I guess I could've gotten him to cross this line earlier if I'd pushed the issue.

My key goes into the lock smoothly, I turn it, and for the briefest second, worry washes over me. Worry that I won't be enough for him. Worry that I'm not as experienced as he is. But then his hand runs from my side up my torso to my bra-covered breasts and his face nuzzles into my neck.

"You have no idea how long I've wanted this," he whispers. "I cannot wait to make that blush spread down every inch of your body."

With his words, I relax and reassure myself that I have nothing to worry about.

He ushers us inside, urging me past the threshold, then kicks the door shut. "No roommates, right?"

"No room—"

He takes the hem of my shirt and pulls it off my body, leaving me in only my bra. "I told you I've been dangling on a thin thread." He smiles, his gaze zeroing in on my breasts. "Even better than I remembered."

I step closer to him, my hand on his chest until his back is against the wall. Our eyes lock with so much lust, it consumes the entire space around us. His breath hitches when my fingers graze down his abdomen and hover over the zipper of his slacks. I lower the zipper and slide my hand inside.

"Fuck," he groans when I take the weight of him in my palm.

His dick is semi-hard and already large. I can't wait to see it, but first I pump my fist over it and he thrusts his hips, wanting more friction. Our eyes haven't left one another's except for every now and then when his gaze dips to my breasts. He struggles to keep his eyes open, and my hand manipulates him until his length is granite hard. And huge.

Oh my god, he's huge.

Guys in porn have nothing on Maksim.

One of his hands rises up my torso at a torturingly slow pace and pulls down the cup of my bra. Then he twists me around, forcing my hand out of his slacks. I expect his hands to go to my breasts, but he slides one down the front of my sweatpants, running a finger between my legs and over my soaked panties.

"This is for me?" his deep voice rumbles in my ear.

I lay my head back on his shoulder, turning slightly to look at him. "Yes."

He slides one side of the fabric over and runs his fingers through the wetness, up and down my folds, before he centers all his attention on my clit.

"Maksim," I say with desperation in my tone.

"Just relax, *kotik*." His free hand grabs my breast, pushing, pulling, teasing my nipple. "I'll feast on these soon."

I feel his thickness poking through his slacks behind me. As if he's frustrated, his hand leaves my breast and I hear his belt buckle release, then I hear it hit the floor as his slacks pool at our feet. I've yet to see it, but the tip of his dick pokes above my ass as his masterful hands shimmy down my sweatpants to join his pants on the floor, leaving me in only my silk panties.

He's perfection in the way he plays with my clit and pussy as though he's been doing it for years, but it's clear he's reading my moans and the arches of my back. Maksim is paying attention to what I like, and there's nothing sexier than that.

"Come on, Paisley. Relax."

I had no idea I'd been holding in any kind of tension, but as soon as he tells me to relax, I release a breath and the pent-up tension releases from my limbs, allowing him to hold my weight while he takes me to the edge. Without thinking, my hand lands on his between my legs, threatening to take over. I'm used to getting myself off, and although he's doing a phenomenal job, I want to make sure I get there. Maksim's all about bringing me to the brink and not letting me fall.

"Hands off, *kotik*," he whispers. "This is my job tonight."

I move my hand up and grab my free breast, twisting my nipple until I shudder in his hold, bucking and crying out while he takes my weight so I don't collapse. Oh my god, that was amazing. Just as I get a hold of my breath, he twists me around.

"Straddle me." He leads me over to the couch by my hand and sits down.

His boxer briefs came off at some point, though I'm not sure when. I get my first look at the perfection that is his Russian cock, and my mouth waters. It's thick and long with a bulbous tip I want to wrap my mouth around. A vein runs the underside, and again I find myself wishing I could trace the outline with my tongue.

"Looked your fill?" He cocks an eyebrow, hands spread out across the back of my couch.

Damn, I know this man could make me his sex slave if he wanted. Have me do his bidding. I stand between his spread legs, and his fingers hook into the sides of my panties and slide them down my legs. I step out of them and climb on my couch, straddling him.

"I should've made you beg." The cutest smile crosses his lips, and I wish I could take a picture. This man has won me over wholeheartedly.

I grind my wetness over him and his head falls back. All I want to do is ride him right now. I want to watch him and know that I'm the cause of his pleasure.

"Do you have a condom?" he asks. "I didn't think to bring one."

"You mean you don't carry them around with you?" I laugh and climb off him, going to my bedroom to grab one out of the nightstand.

When I return, holding it triumphantly in my hand, he bites his bottom lip. "I'm gonna be honest… I'm not thrilled about you having condoms at the ready."

I laugh, ripping open the package. "Oh, well, we could just forget all this." I pretend to walk away, but he snags my wrist, tugging me forward.

"Give me the fucking thing," he growls in my ear.

Giddy with excitement, I hand him the open condom wrapper. He takes it out, and I watch intently as he rolls it down his hard length. I straddle him again, and he guides himself to my opening. I sink down inch by inch. It takes me a minute or two to accommodate the size of him, but then we're both moaning and closing our eyes in sheer pleasure.

I grind down on him, clenching his dick with the walls of my pussy, and every nerve ending inside me lights up.

"Shit, Paise," he says.

His eyes open, a color I've never seen in their depths. They're still as blue as the Caribbean, but it's the deep ocean right now. I thrill at being the one who unfurled that look from him.

He pushes his ass up off the couch, thrusting inside me, and I can tell this isn't going to last long. My breasts shake as I let him set the punishing pace from below me for a minute. Then my hands land on his shoulders and I move up and down as he grabs my ass, widening my ass cheeks apart and increasing my frenzy.

"We're not even done and I can't wait to fuck you again. You've put a fucking spell on me, *kotik*. I can't get enough." His words only spur on my orgasm.

"Oh God, I don't want to come yet. I don't want this to end." I struggle to get a full breath.

But once he urges me up and his mouth covers my nipple, I'm done. I no longer have the control to keep my climax at bay, and I come with his name on my lips.

He doesn't relent, continuing to push into my deepest depths while sweat beads on his forehead. He smashes his lips to mine, his tongue diving into my hot mouth as his body tenses under me.

"Fuck!" Then he goes lax.

Our kiss turns languid and lazy for a while. Eventually I feel him soften inside me, so I slide off of him. He takes the condom and quickly disposes of it in the kitchen. I watch his ass the entire walk over. Then he returns to where I lay spent on the couch, and he runs his fingers up and down my spine.

"Better than I ever imagined," he whispers against my curls.

"Candy time?" I smile expectantly.

He stands, picks me up, and carries me into the bedroom. "Not even close."

I giggle as he slams the bedroom door and tosses me on the bed.

I should've known he'd fuck like a porn star. He's got the dick of one.

CHAPTER 17

"Nice to meet you."

Maksim

"**A**re you ready for our fifth date?" I ask her, sitting on a stool at her breakfast bar.

Last night was crazy. I don't think I've ever had that much sex in one night, but this morning, I could barely make breakfast without thinking about how I wanted to be back in that bed with her.

"Fifth date, huh?" she says, walking out of her bedroom in a shirt that just hits the waistband of her flowy skirt. Her hair is slightly damp, her makeup barely there. She's beautiful as always. "Am I dressed okay for it?"

"It'll do." I shrug.

She stops and stares at me for a moment. "I think I should've held out longer."

She walks past me and I pull her into me, spurring a giggle I'll never get enough of. "You're stunning as always."

"Better." She kisses my cheek. "We have to talk about a few things." Then she's gone from my arms and her tone has changed.

"What do we have to talk about?" I stand and swing my keys around my finger. I ran home this morning to get clothes, and even that felt like it took an eternity.

"The fact I'm your therapist."

I open the front door and she walks through and waits for me to shut the door before she locks it. "I relinquished you."

"Yes, on a notepad, I remember."

"I hear a but?" I open my car's passenger door for her.

"But Mr. Gerhardt doesn't know that. He's still expecting one more session. I'm lucky he hasn't cornered me about it yet because I have nothing to tell him. Nothing that says you'll go easier on the ice." She slides into my car, pulling her skirt all the way in before I shut the door.

I have to tell her at some point about Armen and my past. I don't need a therapist to tell me why I take the role of protector with my teammates. I'm fully aware of why.

"Maybe now that all my sexual frustration is gone, I'll be nicer to those assholes." I shut my door and start the engine.

"Since you can't talk to me, do you want me to refer you out?" Her voice is hesitant, as though she's unsure how I'll react.

"I don't need to talk to anyone. I'm good." I back out of the parking spot and head onto the road.

She says my name as though I don't know myself. I got through Armen's death fine without the help of a therapist. I can get through this too.

"Honestly, I'm good. I'll try to control myself more." I kiss her at the stoplight.

She nods, but we're definitely not on the same page here—she believes therapy is a cure-all and I'm unwilling to open my chest and let my heart fall out.

Fifteen minutes of silence later, we arrive at the location of our date. We'll have to address therapy again, but not today. I don't want to fight.

"Costco?" She stares at the big red sign.

People file out with carts overfilled with large quantities of items.

"The food station?" she asks.

I laugh, turning off the engine. "Better. Samples."

A smile tips her lips, and she shakes her head. "Okay, definitely original, Maksim."

She opens her door and I meet her at the trunk of my car, take her hand, and lead her in.

"It's a secret club," I whisper, while pushing the cart.

"Just your regular ol' speakeasy," she counters, and I laugh. I'm not sure I've ever laughed as much as I do around her. "Why the cart?"

"I have to pick up a few things. If there's anything you want, just put it in the cart and it's on me." I wink and she nods.

"Thanks."

"Don't mention it."

We're clearly being sarcastic, but that's one of the reasons why I love spending time with her.

On the way to the samples area, I grab the protein powder I use for shakes and some chicken. Paisley grabs a bottle of wine and some muffins. We clearly have different priorities at Costco.

Once we get to the food area, there's a sampler out of some taquitos.

"Ladies first." I motion to the tray.

"Oh, how gentlemanly of you." She takes two and feeds me one before eating hers. "What do you think?" she asks after she swallows hers.

"Good. Want to look around a bit more?"

"Sure."

I put some coconut water in the cart, then toilet paper and paper towels. All the stuff I know we've been running low on lately. Paisley peruses the books, reading the backs or inside flaps of each one she picks up.

"Do you read?" she asks while looking at the book in her hand.

"Nope."

"Why not?" She puts down the book, never putting one in the cart.

"I have a lot of shit to do. Relaxing with a book isn't on the top of my list."

"Not even for laying out on the beach?"

I chuckle. "I don't lay out on the beach."

She stops and stares at me as if I'm crazy. "Never?"

"If I'm on the beach, I'm playing volleyball or throwing a frisbee or actually swimming."

"Well, just so you know, if we ever do a beach day, I prefer being lazy and sitting in a lounge chair with a book and some kind of frozen daiquiri in hand."

I pretend to write it down. "Noted."

She puts her arm through mine, kissing me on the cheek. My chest swells at her easy affection. I hope she feels the same about me—that she can't get enough.

We eat some more samples, and she insists on buying a jumbo-sized box of Greek yogurt ice cream treats and I give in like an exhausted dad to a pleading child. "You do know the samples are always better than when you bring them home?"

She shoos me with her hand, putting the box in the cart. "I bet you I'll eat them all within a week."

I read the box. "You're going to eat twenty-four bars in seven days?"

She nods, so sure of herself.

"And if you don't?"

"Why must everything be a challenge to you?" she asks

before thanking the lady giving out chocolate almond samples and inserting one into my mouth.

"What fun is it if there's no reward to the bet?"

"But why must you bet in the first place?"

I snatch her by her waist and pull her toward me. "Because it's fun, and now that our relationship has progressed, we can use sexual favors as rewards."

Her mouth forms an O shape.

"Now you get my point." I slap her ass.

"Are you Maksim Petrov?" a small voice says from behind Paisley.

I look over her shoulder at a little blonde girl with pigtails who most likely just saw me smack Paisley's ass. Great.

I smile and nod. "I am."

Paisley turns around, welcoming the little girl with a big smile. "I love your pigtails."

She nods and her pigtails bounce. "Thank you." She holds out a piece of paper and a pen. "Could you sign this? My dad is a huge fan and his birthday is next week. I heard people saying it was you and I can't get my daddy anything because I don't have a job. Mommy says he likes homemade things and that he'd love a card, but I don't like getting cards. You can't play with a card."

I glance at Paisley, who looks as though she's a second away from cracking up at this little girl.

"This is the back of my mom's grocery list, and if you sign it, I'm gonna make a collage."

I think for a moment. "You'd need proof though, right?"

The little girl's eyes widen. "What?"

"Proof that it was my signature."

Her bottom lip pops out. "My daddy would believe me."

"Oh, I was going to offer a picture, but sure, I can sign." I take the pen and paper, scribbling my name.

"A picture!" Her eyes light up, and I nod. "Let me get my mom."

I catch sight of her mom watching from a distance, so she's not surprised when her daughter takes her hand and drags her over to us.

"Thank you for being so nice," she says when she reaches us.

"Our pleasure. She's adorable." Paisley speaks first, and I like the word *our* coming out of her mouth.

"She really wants to get her dad a gift on her own. I suggested some socks over there, but she said no way."

"I said she could take a picture with me and add it to her collage."

"Oh, that would be great." The mom smiles.

"Daddy will love it." The little girl is already taking the mom's phone out of her purse and handing it to Paisley. "Can you take it?"

"Calm down, Ashley." The mom chuckles, looking a little embarrassed at her daughter's enthusiasm.

I pick up the girl, and Paisley snaps the picture. Once we're done, I lower her back down and Paisley hands the phone back to the mom.

"It was nice meeting you," I say with my hand raised.

Ashley smacks it. "You too. Sorry about the playoffs. Drake kind of screwed you."

"Ashley!" her mother scolds, cheeks turning red.

The girl looks over at her mother. "It's what Daddy says."

The mom gives me an apologetic smile.

"We're not out of the playoffs yet." Though even I can admit that it's a long shot we'd make them now, but never say never. "Give Drake a break. He had a lot going on and his game is back, so I say next year you'll see us win the Cup if it doesn't happen this year." I wink at her.

Ashley nods, still looking unconvinced. I'm not sure how much of a fan she is.

"Thank you again for doing this. It means so much. You're a very sweet man. Not at all like they talk about you when you play." The mom touches my forearm. "And you two make a very attractive couple."

I watch the mom and her daughter leave, and Paisley links her arm with mine. "So that's what it's like to be with someone famous."

I glance over. "They're not all that nice and cute. Believe me."

We leave Costco with more stuff than I thought I'd buy, but that seems to happen to everyone who goes into that place. Since I have stuff that needs to be refrigerated, I figure we'll stop by my house, then figure out what we want to do for the rest of the day.

"Nice shack," Paisley says when we pull up to my beach house.

It's not anything like Drake's, but it's a nice size with four bedrooms, four baths, a pool, and a hot tub. Plus it's right on the beach. I spent way too much for it, but since I'm not some world traveler and kind of a homebody, it suits me well.

"It's not that amazing."

"I think my apartment can fit in your garage," she says, carrying a load of the stuff from Costco into the house.

"I like your place. It suits you."

"I imagined you lived in an ice castle, so this is refreshing," she says, laughing as she walks through the archway of the door.

As I'm making sure the door is shut behind us, Paisley

drops everything in her arms, each item free-falling to the floor.

Nadiya stands in the kitchen, wearing a barely-there bikini. Fuck.

"Oh, hey, I'm Nadiya," she introduces herself with a smile.

"Paisley," she says and looks back at me, eyes narrowed.

"Sorry, my bad. Nadiya, this is my—" I'm not sure how to refer to Paisley, so I look at her.

"Friend," Paisley fills in the blank. "I work for the Florida Fury." She puts out her hand and Nadiya shakes it.

Okay, we're only friends. Irritation creeps up my spine, but I've got a bigger issue to deal with right now.

I drop my boxes on the floor. Nadiya and Paisley both go to pick up the boxes she dropped.

"Nadiya is a friend from back home. I was best friends with her brother for years." I try as best I can to heal the wound I know this surprise has probably caused Paisley.

"Nice to meet you," Paisley says and walks toward the pool Nadiya came from. "What a beautiful view."

Nadiya bites her lower lip and punches my arm behind Paisley's back.

Yeah. I'm a fucking idiot for surprising her like this.

CHAPTER 18

"Take me home and take advantage of me."

Paisley

I try to catch my breath by walking out to the pool. His best friend's sister? Of course, she's a hot blonde with decent-sized breasts and not an ounce of fat on her. Why wouldn't he mention her to me?

My phone buzzes in my purse and it gives me an idea. An easy way out.

It's just a text message from a store about a sale, but I pretend someone called and answer the phone to no one.

"This is Paisley Pearce," I say.

I feel Maksim before he comes into view—an excuse on the tip of his tongue, I'm sure. I have no reason to feel the jealousy that's racing through my veins. She's his best friend's little sister. But why didn't he mention her if it's really nothing? Maybe he wasn't expecting her to be here when we walked in.

"Okay, sure, I can be there in about twenty minutes." I wait, listening to dead air. "See you then."

I hang up and hide my phone in my purse before he can tell there was no one on the other end. I just need some space. Space to figure out this new situation between us and the fact that he lives with someone who could be a runway model.

"Who was that?" Maksim asks, shame coating his features.

"A client. They're requesting an emergency meeting. I'm going to call an Uber." My hand moves to my purse again.

"I'll drive you and you'll let me explain things on the way?"

Of course he wants to clear the air. That's Maksim. He's not one to avoid difficult conversations, other than the reason why he is how he is on the ice. That reason is locked so tight, not even the best safe cracker could get in.

"It's okay, I don't mind."

His hand grabs mine. "Please. I know this must have thrown you for a loop."

I want to scream that of course it did. Why has he never told me he has some kind of roommate situation going on with a gorgeous woman? But is that really any of my business? Maksim's never been anything other than attentive and worn his feelings on his sleeve, and until last night we weren't physical. But I can't help how I feel about the discovery.

"Okay," I say meekly.

Time to buck up, Paisley, and advocate for yourself here.

We walk back through the house and Nadiya holds the box of the yogurt bars in my direction. "I figure these must be yours. He never keeps anything sweet in the house."

"Yep, those are mine." I accept the box. "It was very nice to meet you."

"You should come for dinner sometime. I'd love to get to know the woman who can tame Maksim."

All brain function leaves me for a second as I rewind what she just said. The word *tame* flashes in my head like a neon vacancy light on a hotel on a dark stretch of highway.

"Definitely." I keep my voice as cheery as I possibly can. "Sadly, I have to get to work now. Bye."

"I'll be back, Nadiya. I'm dropping her off." Maksim is following close behind me.

"Sounds good. I'll be sunbathing."

No doubt without her top.

Damn it all to hell, she didn't do anything to me. There's no reason to be catty toward her.

We walk out of the house, and I wait by the passenger door for Maksim to open it, but he doesn't unlock it until he's by my side and his hand is on the door handle. "Question."

I can't even look at him. Tears threaten to fall from my eyes, which would be so embarrassing. "What?"

"Do you really have a client to see?"

"Yeah." I cross my fingers behind my back. I hate lying. Despise liars.

"Look at me," he says. As kind and gentle of a person Maksim is, there's authority in his tone this time, so I obey and look at him. He sees the truth right away. How, I don't know, but he does. "Get in the car, we're going for a ride."

"Maksim—"

"It's bullshit. You have no client. Get in the car." He opens up my door and rounds the back of the car.

"You're not the boss of me."

He stops right before climbing in. "I'm not doing this. I'm not having some stupid fight about a miscommunication between us. I should've told you about Nadiya, I know, but I'm not letting you pretend it doesn't bother you. She will not be the reason things go to shit between us."

I stand there, amazed by this man who can so freely put himself out there. "A please wouldn't hurt."

He stares blankly at me. "Please. Now get in the damn car, *kotik*."

I do as he says because I don't want to feel this way and I am curious why Nadiya is living with him. More than anything, I want to know why he never told me.

I'm barely strapped in when he backs down the driveway.

"Maksim," I say.

"Just wait. I don't want to talk while I'm driving."

I sit in the passenger seat, staring at everything whipping past until we end up on another beach that's more secluded, a lighthouse in view. He gets out without a word, and I open my door, growing agitated that he's somehow taking this out on me. I wasn't the one hiding something from him.

"I'm mad," he says, and that makes me break, my temper coming to the surface.

"*You're* mad? Did you just find out that I have some movie star male roommate living with me who walks around in a man thong all day?" I stomp away from the car to the sand, kicking off my sandals.

"I knew you struggled with trusting me. That someone hurt you. You told me it was your dad, and that's why I've been so cautious and so careful to make sure you knew you can trust me." He comes up alongside me.

"And yet you forget to tell me you have a roommate. A very attractive, very young, very… ugh!" My hands fist at my sides. "You didn't even say anything on the way home from Costco to prepare me, like, 'Oh, hey, I have a hot roommate.'"

"She's not really my roommate. I mean, she is, but she doesn't pay me rent or anything."

My mouth falls open. "And that's supposed to make it better?"

"*Zamolchi!* Just listen to me!" He raises his voice. "Let me fucking explain."

There's a big rock nearby and I climb on top of it. "Fine. Explain."

He huffs as if I'm the one annoying him, then he climbs the rock to sit beside me. "Armen, Nadiya's older brother, was my best friend."

"So I heard."

He stares at me silently until I take the chip off my shoulder, then he continues. "He died when we were just out of school."

My chest squeezes and I blink rapid fire.

"He always looked out for her, so when he passed, I took it upon myself to do the same. Her parents asked me to watch out for her when she decided to come here for school. Our parents are best friends too, and I wanted to make it up to the family, so I offered for her to live with me. Armen's death was hard on all of us."

"How did he die?" I ask.

He focuses ahead of us, staring at the vast water. "It's my fault. I killed him."

"What?" I ask softly, sure I heard him wrong.

"I was driving the car that got into the crash that killed him." He squeezes his eyes shut.

"That doesn't mean *you* killed him. Were you drunk?"

He shakes his head.

"Under the influence at all?"

He shakes his head again.

"Were you texting or distracted while driving?"

He shakes his head. "An animal ran out onto the road and I swerved, then *bam*, a tree was in front of us and that was it."

I close my eyes to center myself. This is Maksim, the protector. "I'm sorry. I should have waited for an explanation before I reacted."

He shakes his head. "I don't think much of Nadiya

staying with me. It's been four years, and she graduates from college this year. Honestly, it's like living with a sister, if I had one. But I understand how it would look to you. Nothing has ever happened between us, nor will it ever." He looks at me with a devilish sparkle in his eyes. "I do like you being jealous though." He slides closer to me and wraps his arm around my waist.

"Who said I was jealous?"

He scoffs. "You were totally jealous, which means you like me. You really like me."

I laugh, almost falling off the rock. "Yeah, I like you. I really, really like you."

Pulling me closer, he presses his lips to my temple. "I'm sorry. I should have prepared you."

"Can I ask you something?" I place my hand on his leg, and he nods. "Have you talked to anyone about Armen's death?"

His smile dims and he releases me, jumping down off the rock. "I don't need therapy. He died, it sucks, life moves on. I'll see him someday when it's my time."

I follow him down off the rock toward the water's edge. "I think it's the reason you try so hard to protect Ford, Aiden, Tweetie, on the ice. I think it's the reason for your misplaced anger."

He looks at me over his shoulder. "Do you think I don't know that? I'm fully aware. And I'm damn good at it. No one will ever get hurt on my watch again."

"Your watch?" My heart aches over the fact that he sees everyone's well-being as his responsibility.

"Yes. But that's not what we're talking about." He smiles and winds his arms around my waist. "I want to go back to your place and ravish you. I feel like I didn't get well enough acquainted with your tits last night."

I'm a therapist, I understand distraction. He doesn't

want to talk about it and there's no way I can continue to see him as a patient—as much of a farce as that was—now that we have a relationship. But it's affecting his job, and in order to move ahead emotionally, he needs to get it all off his chest and have someone help sort through the trauma with him. Sadly, that person can no longer be me.

"I have a great colleague—"

He shakes his head and tugs me, closing the last bit of distance between us. "I want you, *kotik*. Take me home and take advantage of me."

Of course, he's using humor to pretend nothing is the matter. People push their issues to the side all the time and some manage to live happy lives. Surely, it can wait… maybe until the season is over? We're just starting out and I don't want to be the nag girlfriend.

So I let it go. What can it hurt for him to go a little longer without getting the clarity he needs? I ignore the voice in my head telling me that I'm lying to myself.

"Okay." I nod.

His blue eyes widen as though he's surprised by my answer, then he picks me up bridal style and walks us back to his car.

We barely make it back to my apartment with all of our clothes intact. Just after we pass through the door, he tosses the yogurt bars in the freezer, even though I'm sure they're probably totally melted by now, then places me on the kitchen table and falls to his knees. Since I don't cook or have many people over, it's the most action my kitchen table has ever seen.

If only the knot in my stomach wasn't still there, telling me that one day, Maksim's issues with the past are going to come to a head.

CHAPTER 19

"What's the problem?"

Maksim

*P*aisley allows me to distract her from the issue of therapy, for which I'm thankful. I've been this way since Armen died and nothing is going to change. The sooner she realizes I don't need fixing, the faster we can move on from that.

Later that week, I knock on her office door and hear her say, "Come in."

"How's my favorite doctor?" I say, shutting the door and resting my hand on the lock.

She glances up from papers she's reading. "Do not lock that door."

The lock clicks as I turn it, and she gives me a stern teacher look.

"Please don't hurt me," I say in an innocent voice.

"Why do I think you want me to spank you?" She raises an eyebrow.

I turn around and push out my ass. "Have at it. Although I don't think I'm the one who likes to be spanked."

She rolls her eyes, but she can't fight the smile breaking through. I discovered two nights ago that Paisley Pearce likes it when I spank her. Likes when her ass is red with my handprint. How fucking lucky am I? Never in all the years

I've been fucking has a woman surprised me like she has, but she treats missionary like a death sentence. She's kinky as fuck and I love it.

"Do you have a reason you're here? Shouldn't you be, oh, I don't know, practicing?"

"I'll have you know I came to deliver a gift."

"Let me guess." She abandons her papers and walks around her desk. "It's long and thick and its favorite direction is north?"

"Ding. Ding. Dick, tell the lady what she's won?"

Her laughter fills the office. "I think I won dick."

I break the distance between us, wrapping my arms around her small frame and pulling her toward me. "Hey."

"Hey," she says back and looks up at me. "Why are you really here?"

"I'm here to invite you to dinner. Nadiya wants to get to know you. Are you game? If not, I'll totally lie for you."

I try to tamp down my expectations. This Nadiya thing is still new to her, but my parents are coming to America for Nadiya's graduation in a month, and it would be nice if Paisley feels comfortable with more than just me. Especially since they'll probably speak Russian the entire time.

"Okay, when?"

A smile splits my face. I'm surprised but pleased that she agreed so easily. "As soon as we get back from Nashville. The next night."

She nods. "I'll be there. What can I bring?"

"Nothing. I'm going to make you dinner. And bring your swimsuit, because Nadiya is going out after with friends and we'll have the place to ourselves."

"So..." She places her hand on my chest. "Let me get this straight, your roommate is leaving for the night, and you want me to bring my swimsuit?"

I laugh. "*Blyat*, what am I thinking? Bring the swimsuit and I'll punish you."

"With spankings?" she asks coyly.

"Maybe I'll tie you up."

"No objections here." Her hands fall to my track pants.

I'm freshly showered after practice and had planned on heading home before I realized I could play a little doctor and patient before leaving.

Her hand slides down the front and her mouth makes an O when she realizes I'm going commando. "Surprise, surprise."

"Lucky you," I say. "One day I hope to find the same surprise."

"I guess you'll have to keep checking." She pushes me down into her desk chair and falls to her knees. She rubs my length over my pants, squeezing while my fingers grip the armrests of her chair. "I think my gift wants to be unwrapped." Her voice is sultry.

"You have no idea how much," I manage to say through clenched teeth.

She takes the waistband of my pants and pulls it up and over my cock. Her eyes are glued to mine and my dick weighs heavy in her right hand as she licks the length of me.

My hands weave into her long curly strands. "Fuck, *kotik*, that feels incredible."

All I get is a "mmm."

Her eyes never stray as she wraps her lips around the head of my cock and sucks. My hands tighten in her hair. Her tongue twirls over the head and her other hand wraps around the base, pumping as I thrust into her mouth, wanting to get as deep as possible but knowing she can't take all of me.

She works me expertly anyway—twirling, sucking,

pulling, tugging. Even her gentle strokes have me on the edge. Before I realize what's happening, blackness swallows me up as I pump into her mouth and come without warning.

Afterward, my eyes bug open and I look down at her, but my cock comes out of her mouth with a pop and I watch her swallow, a satisfied smile on her perfect lips. How fucking hot is that?

I place my hand on her cheek, running my thumb along her soft skin. "You're amazing."

"I just sucked your cock, of course I'm amazing."

She tucks me into my pants and climbs into my lap. I hold her close, placing my finger under her chin and turning her face toward me so I can kiss her.

"Even if you didn't just blow me, you'd still be amazing." I place my lips to hers and the taste of me on her tongue undoes me. Makes me want to take her to my place and never let her out because lately a new emotion has risen inside me—the fear that I'll lose her for some reason.

"Okay, sweet talker, time for you to go because I have one of your teammates coming in to see me. You know that whole three sessions thing Mr. Gerhardt wants you all to do." She gives me an unimpressed look.

"You'd think now that you're my girlfriend, you'd lie for me." I hold her to my body, wanting to keep her close.

"The G-word… that's a big word." She gets up off my lap and I groan. I've never had it this bad for a woman before.

"Girlfriend? Aren't you?"

She grabs a file folder off the desk and places it over by the chair where she sits during her sessions. "Are you sure?"

"*Kotik*, with the feelings running through me for you, you're lucky I haven't proposed."

She turns toward me and her shoulders fall. I swear she's tearing up. I love that I'm the first guy to ever make her feel as special as she is. It makes me feel ten feet tall.

"Maksim…" She bites her lower lip. "That was really sweet."

"I mean every word of it. Now stop running away from me." I walk over to her and bring her into my arms once more. "Tell me you're my girlfriend."

She nods.

"I need the words."

"Yes, I'm your girlfriend. But we can't tell anyone until I'm not your therapist anymore and I get a chance to talk to Mr. Gerhardt."

"Sign off on the third session then." I raise my eyebrows.

She's reluctant and I have no idea why, other than this notion of hers that I need therapy. "I'll just tell him I'm referring you."

"And then I have to talk to whoever that person is. I don't want to talk to anyone."

She goes still in my arms, her hands on my chest. "I really think you should. Losing Armen the way you did—"

I step away from her. "I'm not talking to someone. End of discussion. I don't need someone to validate my feelings—or worse, tell me I'm not responsible. It is what it is and I don't want to relive it all over again only to end exactly where I am." Even I hear the anger in my tone.

"Fine. But our relationship remains a secret until I have time to talk to Mr. Gerhardt. With the way the season is going, I say we keep this between us until the season is over. I'm sure he'll lighten up then."

"As always, you have brilliant ideas." I move in to kiss her and she lets me, but there's no feeling behind it. I'll have to make up for my outburst tonight. Maybe with my tongue and some whipped cream.

"Now you need to go."

A knock sounds on the door and I look at her with wide eyes.

"Just answer it," she says.

I walk over and open the door to see Mr. Gerhardt.

"Big man, how are you?" he asks. "I'm glad to see you're here. Are you two just finishing up?"

You'd think the owner would know the practice schedule, but whatever.

"Yeah, just finished with my third session." If Paisley won't lie, I will.

"Really? So you're done?" His bushy eyebrows move toward his hairline.

"Technically, our first session wasn't much of one, so I'd like one more with you, Maksim," she says sweetly.

Damn her.

"Sure," I say, inwardly rolling my eyes. Why won't she let this whole situation with Armen slide? He wasn't her best friend. It was ages ago and I've made my peace with it, know what I have to do. I miss him like hell, and I'll never let anyone else get hurt on my watch. She needs to let it rest. "I better get going. Nice seeing you, Mr. Gerhardt. Bye, Dr. Pearce."

Before the door shuts, all I hear is Mr. Gerhardt saying how disappointed he was that she missed the date he set her up on. What the hell is he talking about? Half of me wants to storm in there to demand answers, but I keep my eyes on the door because I can't demand answers when no one knows I've fallen for our team psychologist.

On the way out to my car, my phone rings and I pick it up, seeing my mom's number.

"Mama," I answer.

"Maksim?"

"Yes." I roll my eyes because of my mood. No doubt she'd smack me if she were here to see.

"Nadiya is graduating."

A small smile tugs the corner of my lips. Normally my mother would speak Russian to me, but she always seems to use English before an impending trip to America. I think she uses me for practice. I climb into my Mercedes and hook her up to the Bluetooth.

"Maksim?"

"Yeah, Mama, I'm here. I know Nadiya is graduating."

"We got tickets. I send you our itinerary."

I nod even though she can't see me. "Good."

"You sound sad."

"Nah, I'm good." I leave the parking lot and head toward my place.

"Good. Nadiya doesn't want to come home after school done."

"I know." I've talked about it with Nadiya before, but my mom doesn't need to know that.

"Maybe you find her good job so she can stay?"

"She doesn't want to work for the hockey team, and I'm not even sure I could make that happen anyway."

"I was talking to her mother the other day. We have another solution." I can't wait to hear this. "You marry her."

"What?" I screech, almost swerving off the road.

"Marry her. She's good girl. Our families are close. What's the problem?"

My hands tighten on the steering wheel. "The problem is I don't love her."

"Love. You kids and your love. You love her. Maybe not in love with her, but she's Armen's sister, you love her."

Of course I love Nadiya like a sister, but they're crazy if they think I'm going to marry her.

"She could stay in country. It'd be big favor to her parents. Make everyone happy. Even Armen up in heaven."

"Armen never wanted me near Nadiya. That was clear and I always respected his wishes."

"He'd feel different now. You have success. You give her security and anything she want."

I release a long breath. "I gotta go, Mama. I'll call you in a couple days."

"Don't forget to be at the airport."

"I will. Bye, Mama."

I click off our call and pull over on the side of the road, shoving the car in park. I think she might've been serious. What the hell?

CHAPTER 20

Paisley

*N*ashville is a beautiful city. Especially when Maksim is in my hotel bed. So far, only one Fury teammate knows about us and that's only because he's Maksim's roommate on the road.

This will probably be my last time traveling with the team since almost every player has completed their three sessions. Plus, it's unlikely the Fury are going to make the playoffs, so their season will be ending soon too. I think a handful of the players will choose to continue meeting with me outside of Mr. Gerhardt's requirements, but that will be between us, and nothing to do with the Fury.

"Tonight, after the game, is our sixth date," he says, naked in my bed.

"So tell me, which do you prefer… porn or me before a game?" I lie on top of him, our naked bodies pressed along one another's.

"You, of course."

I kiss him briefly and slide off him. "Now you can have your nap. I have one more session with Tweetie."

"Do you seriously have to go? I nap so much better on your tits." He leans his head on his hand that's propped up with his elbow.

"Sorry, these pillows come with me." I secure my bra and slide on my panties. "But they're yours tonight again."

"About tonight," he says. "Some of the guys got wind and want to come, so we'll have to play it cool."

"Okay." I shrug. It's not ideal, but it will still be fun.

We plan to go on one of those moving pubs where people sit on either side and pedal to drive it around downtown.

"I want everyone to know you're mine. When are we coming out?"

I finish putting on my slacks and blouse, then slide my feet into my heels. "I'm done with the team after everyone has their three sessions. Including you." I tap him on the nose. "So?"

I hate that I've become a nag on this subject. I'm only being a stickler about it because I really think he would benefit from talking to someone. Clearly, he carries a lot of guilt when it comes to Armen.

He rolls his eyes. "Fine."

"I'm just saying, you're the one responsible for us coming out. The sooner I finish everyone's therapy, the sooner I'm not working for the Fury anymore."

"And then you're going back to your private practice permanently."

I hope business picks up or that some of the team continues their therapy beyond what Mr. Gerhardt has required of them. Something to keep the business afloat. Who knows? Maybe next year Mr. Gerhardt will request my presence again. "Yep. So you'll have to hand out your girlfriend's business cards."

"I'll be like Aiden when he's chatting up his girlfriend's skill."

"Perfect." I lean over the bed and kiss him quickly. "Sweet dreams."

He places his hand on the back of my neck and holds me to him, deepening the kiss. God, I can't believe he's mine sometimes. Almost as though it's too good to be true.

*L*ater that night, after the Fury win with a score of two to one, I'm waiting for Maksim and the rest of his teammates to come out of the arena.

It's the first time I've ever waited out here and noticed how many fans linger around, hoping for an autograph or a picture. And it's the first time I've seen how many of the fans are women. No wonder they have the expression puck bunnies.

I feel overdressed in my jeans and an off-the-shoulder blouse. They all have their phones in hand, and I watch as they perk up their breasts and adjust their shirts to show a little more cleavage.

When the door to the building opens, the women murmur to themselves, rising on their tiptoes to get a better view. The deep voices of the team echo into the night air. I wait patiently behind the group, not needing an autograph.

Tweetie comes out first, fist raised and signs a few signatures. He takes a few selfies with some girls but then climbs into the bus to head back to the hotel. Roadie only waves and hands his bag to the bus driver, stepping into the bus without really stopping. A few of the younger guys get swallowed up in the mass of girls. I'm sure they'll be emerging with lipstick on their faces.

Then Ford comes out and stops in front of a group of girls calling his name. He gets pictures with them, and they all hang off him as though they'd welcome an orgy if he made the request.

Aiden and Maksim walk out together. Aiden stops in

front of a boy and his father while Maksim weaves through the crowd with a smile, walking toward me.

Then a girl calls his name. I hear the Russian accent. He turns away from me and she's greeted with the same smile he just had for me. The two of them talk, and I'm stricken by how beautiful she is. Long lean legs, blonde hair, perfect makeup. His face grows serious as he talks to her and she looks at the ground—disappointed, I think. Just as he's about to leave her, she grabs his elbow, thrusts herself at him, and kisses him on the lips.

My eyes widen, but I pretend my heart isn't racing, that I don't want to go over there and rip her off my man. Maksim lightly pushes her away, wiping his face with his forearm. He says something to her in Russian, then walks over to me.

"She kissed me," he whispers when he reaches me, but I'm stricken—and mute apparently.

There are no words for me to say. I can't believe I saw the man I'm falling for in a kiss with another woman, even if he didn't kiss her back.

I nod.

"Let's go." He nods toward the road, drops his bag with the bus driver, and tries to flag down a taxi.

Aiden and Ford are suddenly at our sides.

"Shit, Petrov, the way she smacked those lips on you. I can't believe you turned her down," Ford says, clasping Maksim's shoulder.

Aiden gives me an apologetic look. "Fans overstep all the time."

"But since when does Petrov deny them? I thought for sure she'd be coming with us."

Ford is Maksim's good friend. They hang out after games and during the off-season. I think he knows Maksim pretty well, which means that when Maksim told me he didn't really ever screw the puck bunnies, he lied.

"Shut up, Ford," Maksim murmurs.

Some of the younger teammates join us on the curb with a group of bunnies. Great, this is going to be a fun night.

"I think I'm out. Saige would have my ass if pictures got out in the press." Aiden turns and heads back to the bus. I want to beg him to take me with him.

"You're so whipped!" Ford yells after him.

"And I love it," Aiden yells back, climbing into the bus.

Maksim slides between Ford and me.

"Whoa, I'm with the shrink tonight." Ford swings his arm over my shoulders.

Two taxis arrive, and somehow, I end up in the back with Ford and another player while Maksim rides in the front, the rest of our party following in the taxi behind us. I'm not looking forward to this night anymore.

We end up getting two taverns on wheels. I'm with Ford, Maksim, a rookie, and two bunnies. At least it's not the Russian bunny. Because of the way it works out, I end up between Ford and the rookie while Maksim is between the puck bunnies. It's pure hell, even if they aren't all that handsy and flirtatious. I think maybe they just want to hang out with the team, not get into anybody's bed.

As we're drinking and pedaling, the boys complain about being tired, Maksim more so than the rest.

"How about we hop off and go back to the hotel?" the one girl says.

So much for just wanting to hang with the team.

"Nah. I'm good here." Maksim eyes me over the table.

I sip my beer. "When is your baby due?" I ask Ford because I'd rather engage in conversation than watch these two talk up my secret boyfriend.

Ford balks. "Paisley, we don't talk about my baby mama with ladies present."

I shake my head. "My mistake."

I can't believe this guy is going to be a father.

He leans in and whispers, "Very soon."

I nod. Although the girls were clearly trying to eavesdrop, I don't think they heard.

Since Ford is all about scoring with one of the ladies, I leave him and Maksim to talk with the girls and I set my attention on the rookie. His name is Prescott and he goes by Prez. He was just traded in a few months ago and he barely makes it off the bench. He's originally from North Dakota and has no idea what to do in Florida, so I give him some ideas of places and restaurants to check out.

By the time the night ends and we make it back to the hotel, I'm barely able to keep my irritation in check. This certainly wasn't the date I expected.

I say good night to the group as Ford, Prez, and Maksim walk the girls into the hotel lounge. In the elevator, all I can do is stare at the numbers as the car continues to rise. I know we're not supposed to act like a couple in public, but I could do without Maksim actively flirting with someone else.

As soon as I'm in my hotel room, I strip down and throw my clothes by my suitcase and turn on the water for the shower. I was sweating so badly while pedaling. All I want is to shower and go to bed and not even think about what Maksim is doing.

I'm just about to go into the bathroom when my hotel room door buzzes and opens. Maksim walks in as though he owns the place.

"Excuse me?" I grab a towel to cover myself.

"Why are you covering yourself up?" His eyebrows are raised.

"Um, because I'm naked."

"I've seen you naked."

"How did you get a key for my room?" I change the subject.

"I told them I was your boyfriend. Voilà." He holds up the key card.

"Well, that makes me feel safe."

"Were you disappointed it wasn't Prez? I could call him right now for you." He sits on the edge of my bed and takes off his shoes and socks.

"What? I wasn't the one all over a bunch of puck bunnies tonight."

He looks at me with irritation. "You were talking to him the entire night."

"And you were lip-locked with some Russian chick before the night even started."

"I pushed her off. I didn't ask her to do it."

I stand in the bathroom doorway, waiting for a better answer.

"So what? Prez was payback?" He stands and takes off the rest of his clothes, leaving him in only his boxers.

"What are you talking about? I had a pleasant conversation with the guy while you and Ford chatted up those girls. That's all. Why don't you tell me who the Russian really is?"

He puts his hands on his hips. "She's someone I've seen here before. Her name is Alina."

I suspected as much but hoped I was wrong. "You mean someone you hook up with when you come through Nashville?"

"On occasion. But I told her it was over. That I'm seeing someone now."

I shake my head. "I gotta take a shower."

Heading straight for the shower, I stand under the

stream of water, a million questions accosting my brain and a million emotions swirling through my heart. Does he have hookups in every city? How will I ever deal with his life when I'm not traveling with him? I understand a little better now why it's hard for Saige. Trust is huge and hard for me to give. Do I have what it takes to handle dating a professional athlete? I mean, my dad wasn't famous and look what he did. He didn't have to face temptation from women every time he clocked out for the day.

The fogged up glass door slides aside and Maksim steps in. "We're going to talk about this."

"I'm busy."

"Paisley," he says with a bite.

"Maksim," I impersonate his tone.

"She means nothing."

"Prez was just someone to talk to. I don't like it though. I don't like the girls. I don't like the way it makes me feel." Water streams down my body and I think it's all the better to hide the tears brimming in my eyes.

"Good thing I only like one girl," he says with a smile. He always says the sweetest things. He takes me into his arms, turns me around, and shampoos my hair. "Have I ever told you how much I love your hair?"

"About a hundred times." I allow the distraction, leaning along his body after he's washed and conditioned my hair. I look up at him, feeling more vulnerable than ever. "Maksim, please don't hurt me."

"Never."

Afterward, Maksim dries me off, picks me up, lays me on the bed, and makes love to me—missionary style.

CHAPTER 21

Paisley

I knock on Maksim's door with a cheesecake in my hand.

Nadiya answers in a tight aqua dress that will make sure she's noticed anywhere she goes. She points at the box. "Is that dessert?"

"Cheesecake," I say, offering it.

She takes it from my hands. "I love cheesecake and so does Jessie."

Jesse? Does she have a boyfriend? Maksim is driving me crazy with his lack of details.

Nadiya turns and walks down the hallway toward the kitchen, and I follow. I haven't even been here since I found out about Nadiya.

"He's out on the patio. That man loves to grill." She places the cheesecake in the fridge and turns around, her toes painted the cutest pink.

"I didn't know he grilled," I say, hating that this woman knows more about him than I do.

"Everything from fish to vegetables. Always out on the grill." She waves toward the patio where I'm guessing Maksim is.

He and I have been good. Happy. Still having sex every chance we get. But I can't help but feel as though there's something more going on underneath it all. My jealousy in Nashville. His jealousy in Nashville. Him living with a beautiful woman—regardless of who she is. And Armen. The fact he refuses to talk about his feelings from his friend's death. It's all brewing underneath our new relationship, and sometimes I feel as if we're waiting for a bomb to go off.

"Tell me about yourself. Maks says you're a psychologist? How did you go through that much schooling?"

I laugh. "Well, I love it. I want to help people."

"Good money though. That's what my mama would say. It pays good." She takes a vegetable tray from the fridge and places it in front of me.

"Not yet. Takes a while to get a practice rolling. Hopefully in a few years."

"I'm graduating from a fashion design school and my mama says it's not practical."

"Well, my mom was mad about the loans I took out. I'll be paying those for years to come." I roll my eyes good-naturedly.

"Not if you stay with Maksim." She waggles her eyebrows.

I shake my head. "My bills are my bills."

"That's not how he works." She pours herself a margarita from a pitcher and offers me some, which I accept.

"That's how I'll make sure it works."

She picks up a carrot and points it at me. "Oh, I like you. You've got spine. Inessa will like you too."

I frown. "Who is Inessa?"

"Maksim's mama," she says with a look of concern over the fact that I didn't know that.

In truth, I don't know anything about his family. He

never really talks about them. I guess at this point, I shouldn't be surprised.

"Hey, I didn't hear the door." Maksim walks into the house from the porch, wearing board shorts and no shirt.

I hate that Nadiya sees him like this every day. It's just not a good feeling when another woman knows your boyfriend better than you do, even if their relationship is platonic.

He bends down and kisses me. "Since when do I not get a kiss first?"

"So demanding." Nadiya sips her margarita. "She brought cheesecake."

"You'd think someone told you Nadiya loves cheese-cake." He winks at me before heading to the fridge and pulling out some brown packages.

"Taking credit for something you didn't do." Nadiya refills her margarita and comes over to sit next to me on a breakfast stool while we watch Maksim open the packages of meat. Chicken, steak, and bratwurst.

"Good thing I'm not a vegetarian," I say.

Maksim peeks up at me. "That might've been a deal breaker."

"No, it wouldn't have. He loves you," Nadiya says.

Maksim gives her a look. One that says shut up. A look one might give to a little sister.

Some of the tension coursing through my body relaxes. I'm way too hung up on the fact that Nadiya should be a model for her own fashion designs, rather than the fact that she's just a close friend of Maksim's.

Maksim picks up the plate with all the meat on it. "Come join me at the grill." He waits for me to stand.

"Sure. Are you coming, Nadiya?"

"No, I'm waiting on Jessie." She waves for me to go.

"You guys can have some alone time to make out." She laughs and takes another sip of her margarita.

I follow Maksim out onto his pool deck that overlooks the ocean.

"I didn't see your bag in there?" Maksim says, placing the meat on the sizzling grill.

I sit with my margarita in one of the lounge chairs, stretching out my legs. "It's in the car."

He places the plate down next to the grill, closes the lid, and sits on the edge of my lounger. Leaning down, he rests his forehead to mine. "Hey."

"Hi."

"I've missed you."

"You just saw me yesterday."

"I can't wait to have you alone."

I wind my arms around his broad shoulders. "Me either."

And that's the truth. I love being with Maksim. So much that it scares me. Although I trust him, especially after Nashville, when I witnessed his own insecurities with our relationship. He was afraid of losing what we have too. I know this—us—means something to him.

We sit like that for a while, listening to the waves.

"I'm thinking sex on the beach tonight?" he whispers.

"Sounds good to me."

He rises moments later to check on the meat and I watch, thankful to have scored a guy like him. Besides putting his feelings for me out there, he's nice to look at. His muscled back flexing as he turns over the meat. His perfect V shape that tapers down to his waistband. The man really is an Adonis.

"Jessie's here!" Nadiya calls, joining outside with a woman at her side.

Who I thought was Jesse is actually Jessie. She's a short-haired brunette with tattoos sprinkled all over her body. She's wearing a tank top and a short fluffy skirt, and her eyes are as sparkling blue as Maksim's. She's very pretty.

"Hey, Jessie," Maksim says.

"Hey, big guy." Jessie rises onto her tiptoes to kiss him on the cheek. She turns around and sets her gaze on me, a smile on her lips. "So this is the girl you've been cheating on me with. Nice."

"Sorry, but she prefers what's under my shorts," Maksim says, and they both laugh.

Nadiya sits next to me on the lounger, nudging me to scoot over even though there's a perfectly good empty lounger next to me. "Maksim doesn't understand lesbians." She chomps down on another carrot.

"I understand them just fine. I understand wanting tits and pussy over some dick. Especially when it comes to my girl." He winks, and I cross my legs as Jessie's gaze settles on me.

I finally clue into the dynamic and what it means. Once again, I feel like an idiot because I've been kept out of the loop.

"She's very cute, like the girl next door," Jessie says. "But I bet she's kinky."

Jessie sits in the lounger next to me, and Nadiya quickly swaps out mine for hers. She gives Jessie a quick kiss, and Jessie holds Nadiya to her body much like Maksim does to me.

"You really need to learn how to fill a girl in," I say to him.

Nadiya sits up. "He didn't tell you I was a lesbian?" She looks at Maksim as he shrugs.

"It's not my business to tell. Besides, I didn't see why it mattered. If Paise trusts me, she trusts me, regardless of whether the girl living with me likes dick or not."

Nadiya and Jessie look at one another.

"You were testing her," Jessie says exactly what I was thinking.

"No, I wasn't." He disappears inside with the dirty tray.

"Don't be mad at him," Nadiya rushes to say to me. "He just wants to make sure you two can deal with the groupies who don't understand the word no."

"Don't make excuses for him," Jessie tells Nadiya, shaking her head.

"I'm not. But you know how jealous girls get when they're dating. It's the number one reason for their breakups—the insecurity of not being enough for him." Nadiya softens her expression as if saying, "You understand how it can be."

All I can think about from what she said is how many other girlfriends he might have had. I want to scream. What the hell is wrong with me? I've had boyfriends too. Of course he's had girlfriends. We both have a past. But I don't want to think about any of that because in my head, he's mine.

Maksim comes out and interrupts our conversation, carrying a clean dish to put the meat on. He barely looks at us until he takes everything off the grill. "Let's eat so these two can leave and I can have you all to myself."

Nadiya smacks him on the back, and we all file inside to prepare our plates.

The conversation over dinner is enjoyable and I enjoy getting to know Nadiya and Jessie a bit more, even if I'm pushing my irritation with Maksim to the back of my head the whole time.

After we eat, all four of us sit around the pool. Nadiya tells me how her relationship with Jessie started when they met in a class and how they're developing a clothing line together. Watching them is like looking through a peephole you can't look away from. They're so cute together, and it's clear to see why they're a couple.

"But first things first, we need to get Nadiya to stay in the country after her school visa is finished." Jessie sets her eyes on me as if I have some sort of control over it.

Maksim tenses at my side. I place my hand on his thigh because I'm sure she's been a part of his life for so many years now, it would be hard for him if she had to return to Russia.

"What can you do?" I ask with concern.

"Marry Maksim." Nadiya laughs.

So does Jessie. I giggle but notice that Maksim doesn't. For the umpteenth time with him, I feel as if I'm missing something.

Nadiya throws her napkin at Maksim. "Stop being like that. It would never come to that."

I turn to look at him. "What are they talking about?"

"This is when I'm happy I'm a lesbian. Girls can't keep secrets." Jessie stands. "I'm going to get the cheesecake." She heads inside, but Nadiya stays outside with us.

"Maksim?" I raise my eyebrows.

Nadiya grabs my hand to divert my attention away from Maksim. "Our mamas have this crazy idea that Maksim should marry me so I can stay in the country, but don't worry. That's not going to happen." She laughs as though it's funny.

"Oh."

"No. No. No. Don't you go thinking either one of us would entertain such a crazy idea. Our mamas just want to keep us both here and they'll do anything to make it happen. Who knows, maybe I'll marry Jessie." She smiles, and I can see in her eyes that she's hopeful that might come to pass.

"They don't even know you're a lesbian, Nadiya. You'd have to tell them that first." Maksim sips his beer, looking disinterested in the conversation.

"Didn't you think you could tell me?" I ask him.

"I better go help with the cheesecake before Jessie eats it all. She has a huge sweet tooth." Nadiya leaves us.

I stand without a word and walk toward the beach, unsure how to take this news. Standing on the edge, I slip off my shoes and let my feet sink into the sand. Maksim joins me moments later with a new beer and a fresh margarita for me.

"Why do you keep things from me?" I walk down the beach, and he joins me.

He says nothing for a moment. "If it makes you feel better, I've told you more than I've ever told anyone."

I stop walking and he turns to face me.

"That information is something I should've known."

"Why? I'm handling it."

"But I'm your girlfriend. You're supposed to share things with me."

"My mama's crazy plan for me to marry someone she doesn't even know is a lesbian?"

"You hid her from me to begin with, then you allowed me to think she was straight."

"So?" He sips his beer.

"It's deceitful, and I think you were testing me. Would you like it if I tested you?"

He places his beer down on the sand and grabs my glass, setting it next to his. "I didn't mean to test you. I just forgot about Nadiya in the first place, and I do think it shouldn't matter whether she's straight or not. I want you to trust me. I know it's a big thing for you after what your dad did. If I told you she was a lesbian right away, you never would've had to deal with your jealousy. And I need to know that you can, because it's been an issue with women I've seen before. I'd rather know early on rather than down a long stretch of road. But after Nashville, I get it. I can be jealous too, and I hate that fucking feeling. And it scares me because it means I'm not just falling for you, *kotik*, I've already fallen."

Jesus, this guy. He's got an answer for everything, and he always wins me over.

Warmth fills my chest. "I've fallen too. But, Maksim, I want you to go to therapy so we can be out in the open."

He nods. "Okay."

I'm not sure if he agreed just to end this tiff we're in and have a pleasurable night, or if he really is going to stop fighting me on it.

Either way, he takes me in his arms and walks us into the ocean, through the waves that retreat back into the deep dark sea. All I can think is that I wish they could take all our problems with them.

CHAPTER 22

"Surprises are never good unless it's their birthday,
an anniversary, or a proposal."

Maksim

*M*alcolm has become a great skater. I've been able to teach him how to do a slap shot while he's standing in front of the net, but he still struggles with stick handling when he's on the move. But our first game isn't for a few weeks.

"I don't understand why I have to be the goalie." Dru skates out wearing all the pads. "How do I even stop a little black puck I can't see?"

Roadie calls the kid over. Since we have a long way to go, I recruited a few teammates to help out. Tweetie's got Marin. Aiden's got Lark. I'm handling Malcolm. Poor Paisley has everyone else who's taking a bit longer to get the feel of the skates.

During our break, I skate over to Aiden. I'm sure Paisley and I are just going through normal relationship problems, but I want his advice because I don't enjoy these little tiffs we keep finding ourselves in. Except for the makeup sex.

"You available for a drink after?" I ask.

"Sure. Why?"

"We'll talk about it then."

I steal the puck away from him because I don't want

him to corner me here with Paisley's eyes on us. He skates after me, and before I know it, all the Fury members are having a little game of pick up. Roadie gets in front of the goal when Tweetie skates near it and almost scores.

I forgot how fun hockey is when you're not playing for a living. Not that I don't love it, I do, but not having the pressures of ownership, coaches, and fans is a nice change too.

The kids get a kick out of watching us. Each one cheers on the player who's been helping them the most, which only gets our blood pumping.

"Look at the way they skate backward like it's nothing," Malcolm says.

"And the fact you can barely see where the puck is," Lark comments back.

I can't speak for the other guys, but the kids going on about our skills only drives me harder to score, to be the one they all love. None of us have pads on though, so we're going easy on one another. When we finish, the kids join us, asking a million questions, and I'm out of breath and head to the bench.

Paisley hands me a water. "Impressive. I like seeing you having fun out there."

I look at her. Her dark hair is pulled back in an unruly bun, and her wide smile deepens her dimples. I don't think she meant anything by her comment.

"What do I look like when I'm playing?"

She stares at me, and I already know I won't like the answer. "Normally?"

"Yeah." I nod.

"Angry. Pissed off. You have to be because you're playing a role out there, right?"

Suddenly something clicks. Gerhardt wanting me to

loosen up. The fans thinking I'm scary. The opposing team's fans hating me. But I enjoy going out every game, don't I? *Blyat.* Maybe I don't—I sure as hell don't feel happy like this after a Fury game.

After the kids are driving away on the bus, Aiden and I head to Carmelo's.

We take a corner booth and order our meals. Since game day is tomorrow, I opt for a chicken meal with a side of pasta, and Aiden decides on the same. I forgot how in sync we were before Saige came into his life and Paisley into mine.

"We're not making the playoffs," he says, staring at his water with a frown.

"Stop feeling sorry for yourself. You had a bit of a bad run, but you bounced back. You don't carry the whole team on your shoulders. We've rebounded well this last bit of the season."

He nods. "You know Gerhardt will make trades, get some new guys in for next year."

I nod. I hate it, but it's the nature of the business. If I don't watch myself, I might be one who gets traded.

"You assholes hiding out from me?" Ford comes to the edge of our booth and motions for me to slide over.

"We're talking about relationship shit. Stuff you don't care about," I say, hoping Ford will leave. I didn't invite him because he won't give me any valuable advice and he doesn't know about my relationship with Paisley.

He feigns insult. "Excuse me, but I'm about to have the most meaningful relationship possible in a few weeks."

"And thankfully that little one has a mom who will

really take care of him or her." Aiden raises his glass and I tap it with mine.

"You guys are assholes. You watch. I'm gonna be a DILF. The dad all the women wanna fuck."

Aiden laughs. "You know you have to change diapers, feed the baby, stay up with the baby. You don't just get visitation to stroll around the park with the baby to pick up women?"

Ford narrows his eyes. If I'm honest, I think he has what it takes to be a good dad, but it's gonna take a come to Jesus moment for him. Maybe once the baby is born and he holds his offspring for the first time.

Still, I guarantee the mother will be doing the brunt of the child-rearing. Ford's been going back and forth to New York to attend the doctor's appointments with his one-night stand. His mom is over the moon and his dad is still pissed off. But once that baby comes, Ford's life is gonna change. I hope he's ready.

"Of course I know that. Don't worry, I'll have a hot nanny too."

Aiden shakes his head. The waitress comes over and takes Ford's order. I don't really want to talk about Paisley now, but I have no choice because we all live busy lives and I want to smash these small barriers that keep popping up between Paisley and me for good.

"What's the secret meeting about?" Ford asks, opening the conversation.

"I'm dating Paisley," I say to him and point. "And you cannot tell a soul. No one."

"The hot therapist? Damn, I wanted to nail her too, but thought she might be a little prudish for me."

"Shut the fuck up, Ford, and listen," Aiden tells him.

If he only knew her sex drive is as insatiable as mine

and that the only time I've gotten her in missionary was when I made love to her in Nashville. Both of us needed to feel that connection between us.

"Anyway, we're starting to have these little fights. Like about Nadiya and stuff."

Aiden nods. "I'm not sure Saige would've been cool about a hot blonde living with me."

"But she's a lesbian, so who cares?" Ford shrugs.

"I never told Paisley that."

They both stop drinking and glance at me, then at one another.

"Why not?" Aiden asks.

I shrug.

"Fess up," Ford says.

These two guys know me better than anyone. Probably even better than Armen did when he was alive. So I say, "You know all the shit we deal with… how everyone thinks we fuck around all the time and any time we get a girl-friend, they can't handle life on the road, the puck bunnies always hanging around…"

Aiden nods.

Ford, surprisingly, doesn't say anything. Although he's kind of a playboy, he's not nearly as big a one as the press makes out. And he doesn't have a girlfriend, so he's free to do what he wants.

"I didn't want to be invested in her and have it all blow up because she couldn't deal. I wanted to see how she'd react. I was gonna tell her though, and does it really matter in the end?"

Aiden laughs. "Man, I thought you could handle a woman, but it turns out you suck. Honesty and open communication." He holds up his two fingers. "You need those for a relationship to survive. Even if you think she doesn't need to know, she does. Whether it's why you bought a different brand of toilet paper or why she doesn't need to be concerned that you live with another woman. Tell her that shit before she finds out. Because she'll always find out."

"You're even more whipped than I thought. What the hell, man?" Ford says.

Aiden isn't apologetic about it though. "Surprises are never good unless it's their birthday, an anniversary, or a proposal."

I blow out a breath.

"You have to put yourself in their shoes," Aiden continues. "What if she had some hot guy living with her and failed to tell you he's gay?"

"I'd be pissed," I say. Listening to Aiden and looking back, I realize I'm the cause of most of our relationship hiccups. "My mama wants me to marry Nadiya to keep her in the country."

Both of them freeze mid-sip of their drinks.

"Yeah, you heard me, and I didn't tell Paisley that either. Nadiya did."

Ford shakes his head. "You're worse at relationships than me."

"You don't have relationships," I remind him.

"True." He leans back in the booth.

"If I were you, I'd apologize and tell her everything. Getting through things together is what's going to make you strong enough to remain together when the next thing comes along. If that's something you're worried about, just get it all out in the open." Aiden is a straight shooter, and that's why I appreciate having him as a friend.

"Yeah, maybe."

"You like her though, huh?" Aiden asks, and Ford studies me.

"I really do." I sip my drink.

Ford looks between Aiden and me. "How did I not know you're fucking the team shrink?"

My hand squeezes tighter around my drink. "I'm not fucking her, I'm dating her."

"And you're fucking her," he says pointedly.

I shrug. He has a point.

Ford throws his hands in the air. "Great, now you're both done for. What the hell am I gonna do now?"

Aiden and I laugh.

"What you always do. Go out, drink, and party," I say.

"But you guys keep me in line." He frowns.

The food comes and we all dive in.

"I guess you'll have to keep yourself in line." I raise an eyebrow at Ford.

"We'll prepare ourselves to see your name in the media a helluva lot more," Aiden says around a mouthful of food.

I laugh.

Ford doesn't. He knows this could mean more trouble. We've both helped keep him in check. Lena, his family's publicist, might just have to hunker down in Florida until he gets his act together.

After we finish, we head out to a driving range. Might as well start working on our golf game since we're not making the playoffs.

As I watch the small white balls sail through the air, I think of all the balls I have up in the air. Nadiya and my parents' insistence that I marry her. My parents' visit in a few weeks and introducing them to Paisley. The therapy Paisley keeps demanding I go to. After today and how I felt on the ice when we were just messing around, I think maybe I should talk to someone about Armen.

What happened to my easy life? The one where I played hockey, chilled on the beach, and got laid every so often? Where my mind wasn't consumed with a certain brunette and how our future would pan out? Those were the good old days, because I'll never get Paisley out of my head now. She's seared her name onto my heart like a brand whether I wanted her to or not. Now I have to figure out how to make us work for the long haul.

CHAPTER 23

"This doesn't look good."

Paisley

I'm in Mr. Gerhardt's suite again for a home game, and I can't get this feeling in my gut to go away. We're playing Warner Langley's team, and usually when the Fury plays against him, Maksim follows Langley as though he's his shadow. I've heard rumors about some kind of bad blood between Ford and Langley, but I've never asked Maksim about it. I sit as close as I can, wishing I could be in the front row to somehow rein Maksim in.

"You've been busy," Jana says, sitting right next to me.

"I know. I'm sorry."

"Don't be sorry, just give me the details so I can live vicariously through you."

I laugh. If she only knew how many times I've wanted to live her life over the years. "Not much to say. Just spending a lot of time with you-know-who."

"A lot is an understatement. Are you guys, like, living together now?" She sips her martini, then twirls her stick with three olives around in the vodka.

"No. Stop it." I keep my gaze on the ice, waiting for the inevitable.

"You can't even take your eyes off of him for one second." She laughs, leaning back and crossing her legs. "Did you see this guy my dad has here tonight?"

I glance over my shoulder. "Is that Kane Burrows?"

Damn, he's even finer than I remember. He has a full beard and chin-length brown hair that has a bit of a wave to it. Kane played professional hockey until this season, when he didn't get signed by a team. Word is that he had something personal going on in his life and lost focus. I wonder if he's here hoping to play for the Fury next year.

"That would be him, and man, is the guy arrogant."

"Hot though." I raise my eyebrows at her.

She rolls her eyes. "And he knows it."

Just before I look away, I catch Kane glancing in Jana's direction, his gaze lingering on her body. Huh.

Then I return my attention to the ice as Maksim nails Langley against the boards again. This results in Maksim's second penalty of the night, and we're only in the first period.

I continue talking to Jana a bit about Maksim, not divulging my weariness over him hiding things from me. I can't share that much with her here for fear of someone overhearing us.

In the second period, I cringe when Maksim trips Langley, giving Maksim his third penalty of the night.

"He better watch it or he's out for the game," I whisper.

Jana's hand lands on my forearm. "You know you can't control him, right? You can't control how he plays out there," she says in a low voice so no one overhears.

I stare at her hand. I guess I am that transparent. "I know."

"Then calm down. Whatever he does is his own problem."

Oh, how nice it would be if that were true. But I care for Maksim. I want him to talk about his issues so he can enjoy hockey again and not feel pressured to right every wrong that happens out on the ice. It's not good for him emotionally or for his career. I'm pretty sure he gets on that ice with one mission—to make sure everyone knows they can't fuck with any of the Fury or they'll have to answer to him.

But I saw the look on his face when he was with the Fury Juniors. When he was skating with his friends just to skate. It was a side of him I've never seen when he's playing a Fury game. I understand that there are enforcers in hockey, but Maksim takes it to a different level. He needs to let go of his guilt about Armen's death.

But I can't force the man to seek out help he doesn't want. Part of me thinks I should just sign off on his therapy so we can come out as a couple. I've been holding it over his head for so long and he's yet to even ask for a referral.

Maybe Jana's right. I can't control the way he is. Either I love him for him, or I end whatever we have if I can't deal with it.

As I'm coming to the realization that I need to stop pushing therapy on him, Maksim charges another player, earning his fourth penalty of the night. One more and he's out of the game.

"See what I'm talking about? We're barely in the second and there he goes again. He needs to stop giving the other team power plays," Mr. Gerhardt says from behind me, Kane Burrows beside him.

Jana pretends not to notice Kane, which is her telltale sign that she finds him attractive. Not that I think she'll ever admit it. He's not her usual type—he's much too rough around the edges and burly for that—but he is definitely nice to look at.

"That's his job. I'm a firm believer in having an enforcer on the team. Keeps your top guys like Drake and

Jacobs free of injury if he does his job right." I like Burrows's thought process. He shares the same one as Maksim.

Maksim gets out of the penalty box, and I see the look in his eye when I look at the Jumbotron. Even the announcers on the TV behind me say how pissed Maksim is after a bad call by the referee. I might as well just wait for him to get ejected.

Aiden has the puck down by our end and Maksim is weaving in front of Langley to make sure he can't get to the puck.

"Here he goes," I whisper.

Knowing Maksim's number now, another player on Langley's team distracts Maksim. Langley's skates leave the ice and he clips Aiden, but the refs don't see it. What the refs miss, Maksim doesn't. He hip checks the guy they brought in to distract him from Langley, skating toward his original target. Maksim rises off his skates and pounds into Langley, making him fall to the ice and almost crash into the boards headfirst.

The refs blow the whistles and the crowd roars.

I close my eyes, not wanting to see what's about to happen. Peeking one eye open, I see Maksim fling his arms out to get the hands of his teammates off him. He walks off the ice and down the hallway to the locker rooms, knowing he's out for the game.

I blow out a breath.

"I guess therapy didn't work, huh, Paisley?" Mr. Gerhardt puts his hand on my shoulder.

I stand and round the back of my seat. "Apparently not."

And that's the truth. He's gone and gotten himself ejected. How the hell is he going to protect his boys from the locker room? I know that's what matters to him.

"I have someone I'd like to introduce you to," Mr. Gerhardt says to me.

I blink at his quick change of subject. "Another fix-up?"

"What can I say? I find guys that are your type all the time, and since my daughter doesn't allow me to fix her up, I choose my second daughter."

Mr. Gerhardt is always making me feel like a part of their family, which I normally appreciate. Just not in this instance. "My schedule is pretty booked."

"One night out won't kill you."

I smile politely, not wanting to make a big deal of it in front of all these people. "Can you excuse me? I need to use the restroom."

I leave the suite and head down to the locker rooms, showing security my employee pass. Nudging the door open a little, I find Maksim stripping off his pads and throwing them into his locker.

"Maks?" I say.

He turns to me, the anger softening on his face. "What are you doing here?"

"I came to check on you." I look behind me and step inside, closing the door.

"I'm fine. Fucking refs don't call shit. What are they being paid for?" He tears off everything, leaving him in just his jockstrap. He sits on the bench in front of his locker and throws his head into his hands, his hair slicked with sweat. "I'm sick of being the only one who sees this shit."

I hear a television with the game on in the next room. I wish I could go turn it off. He just needs to chill at this point.

I stand in front of him, putting my hands on his head. He widens his legs and pulls me into him, snuggling his face into my stomach and clenching the back of my shirt.

This poor man and the burden he carries with him every game. I wish I could ease some of the load for him.

His hands inch my shirt up, his lips pressing to my stomach.

"Maksim," I sigh. It feels good, but we're in the locker room where anyone could walk in at any time.

"Shh…" he says, unbuttoning my jeans and sliding them down my legs.

Even though I know I shouldn't, I let him. His finger slides the crotch of my panties over and runs along my folds while his other hand snakes up my shirt and grabs a hold of my breast.

"I need you so fucking bad." He pushes my jeans down the entire way, so I step out of them and he hoists me up, my legs wrapping around his middle.

God, he feels incredible. The calloused tips of his fingers massaging my ass, his hot, wet kisses along my collarbone. As much as I feel as though I should push him away, I can't.

He gets my back up against a locker and shifts to hold me in one of his arms while he frees himself from the jock-strap. Teasing me with the tip of his hard cock, he runs it through my wetness.

"Condom?" I ask.

"I'm clean."

I bite my lip. I'm on the pill. I was waiting to tell him until we were at that stage of our relationship, but I'm not sure I can hold out. We have an entire period before that team will come in here.

"Me too, and I'm on the pill."

He doesn't even acknowledge my words before he pushes into me, making me lose my breath. His dick fills me completely. Nothing has ever made me feel more like his than when he looks me in the eye with such conviction when he's inside me. As though I'm the one who can change his mood. Remove his burdens. Make him happy or sad. The man's eyes give away every feeling inside him, and I close mine briefly with the knowledge of what we are to one another.

"Goddamn, you feel so good, *kotik*." He's doing most of the work, so I pull my T-shirt behind my head and pull down my bra straps, wanting and needing his hot mouth on my nipples. As soon as they're free, he's there, licking, sucking, and nibbling.

"Don't stop. Please don't ever stop."

"Never, *krasavitsa*. Never."

I love when he uses Russian words for me. I don't know what they all mean, but I know I'm the only one in his life that he uses them with.

He growls into my neck and my back hits the lockers over and over. It's noisy, but I don't care. We're both chasing the high of what we are together. I wrap my arms around his neck, needing to ground myself to get max enjoyment. His head is in my breasts and he's switching his attention from one to the other.

Sweat forms between us, and murmurs of swear words and praise for one another leave us both. I use my legs around his hips as leverage to help him with the momentum that's going to have each of us screaming in a moment.

Just when I think my orgasm will never crest, it's like a rogue wave crashes into me. Maksim doesn't let up, pumping into me until his hips jerk one final time and he pushes his face into my neck. After we both come, we don't move or talk. We're exhausted and breathless as he stands there, holding my weight.

On the television, the announcers are talking about

Aiden racing with the puck down the center, passing to Ford, who passes back.

"Here comes Langley," one says, and Maksim tenses in my arms.

"This doesn't look good," the other announcer says.

"And Langley nails Drake to the wall, and Drake is down."

I lower my legs and Maksim sets my feet on the floor before he leaves me to go watch the television.

"This isn't good. The way these two teams play, lambasting one another. I think we knew when Petrov left the game Langley would use it to his advantage."

I get dressed while listening and hear medics being called out to the ice. By the time we're both dressed and walking out of the locker room, Aiden is unconscious and being wheeled out of the arena.

CHAPTER 24

"She's way too good for an asshole like you."

Maksim

I rush out to the ambulance as they're wheeling Aiden into it. He's just lying there lifeless.

Saige sits in the ambulance, holding his hand and whispering to him. "It's okay, baby, come on. Wake up."

An arm wraps around my shoulders. Paisley. Sweet Paisley, but even she can't get me out of this.

I grab the arm of one of the paramedics. "I'm coming to the hospital. Which one are you taking him to?"

"He'll be at Memorial," he says.

"We'll be right behind you, Saige," Paisley tells her, but her eyes never leave Aiden.

The ambulance leaves with the lights and sirens, and suddenly I'm back on that highway in Russia, watching Armen being loaded into an ambulance.

The police were using flashlights to stare into my eyes, asking me to walk a straight line, recite the alphabet backward. They were sure we were drunk, but an animal had come out and I swerved, lost control, and hit a tree. To them, we were just two teenagers who were driving crazy.

"Is he okay?" Armen's blood-curdling cries as they extricated him from the car were still ringing in my head. At least he was breathing, I thought. Maybe all the blood didn't mean it was as bad as I suspected.

"They'll get him to the hospital. Let's get you situated," the police officer said. "Take you down to the station."

"Come on, Maksim, let's go." Paisley is pulling on my arm to get me to move. I do, and she wraps her arms around my waist. "This isn't your fault. This is just hockey. Part of the game."

"Let's just go," I say grimly.

I dislodge her from my body and run inside to get my shoes and my keys. Within five minutes, we're in my Mercedes and heading to the hospital as I pray like hell I'm not responsible for the death of another best friend.

We're not allowed back to see him, which I should've expected. I'm just a friend. I wasn't allowed in with Armen either.

Paisley does most of the talking with the nurses, her demeanor much friendlier than mine. We sit in the waiting room, my knee bouncing nonstop as we wait for some news. Anything.

Saige comes out a little while later. "He's awake."

Paisley hugs her. "Thank goodness. Oh good."

"But he has to go in for surgery." Paisley leads Saige over to a chair as she keeps talking. "A ligament in his shoulder is damaged, plus he has a concussion, which is why he blacked out. But he knew who he was, who I was. That's good news, right?" She's asking Paisley as though she's a medical doctor.

Paisley nods, but she has no idea. Armen had surgery too.

"They're taking him into surgery. Internal bleeding," his mama came out to tell us. I felt her eyes on me, silently asking if we were driving too fast, too reckless, and much like the police, had we been drinking or using.

Armen and I weren't the best sons in the world. We lived our lives fast, thinking we were invincible. So her assumptions weren't off base.

But this time, we'd been innocent. We'd just been talking about where life would take us. I'd been drafted into the NHL, but Armen hadn't. He didn't know if he wanted to come with me to America or not.

He was a better man than me, because he always seemed happy for my success with hockey. I'm not sure I would've if our roles had been reversed.

"I'm sure he's going to come out of this." My mama led her to a chair, trying to inspire hope in her.

His dad had gone outside to smoke, and Nadiya was slouched in a chair, having been woken by the police knocking on their door.

More of our friends came. Other families filled the waiting room. Food and drinks were brought in, since we knew we'd be there the entire night.

"Maks." Paisley's soft voice rings in my ear. "Wake up. Some of the team is here."

I shake my head. How the hell did I fall asleep with all the adrenaline coursing through my body?

"I'm going to fucking kill Langley next time I see him." Ford paces the floor. "How much money do you need for me to get back there?"

"Sir, again, you're not family," one of the nurses says.

Saige returns to the waiting room. "His parents and sister will be flying down first thing in the morning." She sits down and brings her nails to her mouth.

"And to think Gerhardt is giving you shit for being an enforcer. You're out of the game and look what happens," Ford says to me.

"Exactly. I wasn't in the game. I fucked up." I stand and look out the window of the hospital. The rest of the world looks dark and asleep.

"It's not your fault," Paisley says.

"Then whose fault is it?" I yell, whipping around with my arms outstretched at my sides.

She steps back, shock on her face.

"I was supposed to be there. To nail Langley before he nailed Aiden. It's my job, my responsibility, but I got myself thrown out of the fucking game. Gerhardt is right. If I'd been calmer, I would've still been in the game, but I'm losing control of everything."

I push my hands through my hair. Paisley puts her hand on my forearm, but I fling it off.

"I just need to be alone."

I grabbed my dad's cigarettes and went out to the front of the hospital, sat on a bench, and smoked one after the other. I knew internal bleeding was never a good thing, and the surgery was taking forever. I couldn't control my guilt over my best friend fighting for his life because I'd swerved and lost control. It was all my fault that he was up there, maybe taking his final breath.

"Son." My dad came out and sat next to me, holding out his hand for the pack of cigarettes. I gave them to him. "This isn't going to help you once you get to the pros."

I shrugged. "What if—"

He shook his head. "We don't think of what-ifs. We wait and see what is."

My dad was a sensible man. Always had been. He'd pushed, as had Armen's dad, for us to be the best at hockey. Our dads had played in the men's league and took hockey to a different extreme. There were no rules. Just as my dad had been a defenseman, so was I. Armen's dad had been a center, which made it so much harder for Armen to go professional. It's like shortstop in baseball—everyone wants to be one. Not that Armen wasn't a kick-ass center, but had he been a defenseman, maybe he would've made it.

"He could be paralyzed," I say.

"He could, but we don't know." My dad lit his cigarette. "This isn't your fault. This was an accident."

I nodded as if I agreed, but we both knew I didn't.

"Maybe I shouldn't go to America. Armen will need me here to help him heal."

We were like brothers. We'd grown up together, fought like brothers, protected one another like brothers. I was already on the fence about leaving him behind since he didn't know if he'd join me. It just didn't feel right. I'd come back from America to visit and he'd be playing in the men's league and working a regular job. I couldn't stand the thought of us losing touch.

"Armen has plenty of people here. You are leaving."

In my family, what my dad said went. You didn't argue. But if Armen was paralyzed, I was staying in Russia. But I would do what my dad asked and wait until we knew what was.

"*Y*ou can't talk to her like that." Jana comes up to me by the vending machines. I'm not even sure why I'm here when I'm not hungry. "She's trying to help you."

"Thanks for the advice."

She shoves my shoulder. "We get it, okay? You feel responsible, but pushing away the girl you love isn't going to accomplish anything."

"Love?" I question with a laugh. "Who ever said I loved her?"

I'm being cruel. I know it. This is what happens when I'm faced with things I can't control. I get spiteful and mean, and I hate that Paisley's friend is seeing this side of me. If only I could control it.

"Do you want me to kick your ass right here?" Jana tosses her purse and jacket on the floor as though she plans on doing just that.

"I'd like to see you try."

"Jana," Paisley says from the doorway. I have no way of knowing if she heard me or not, but from the look of gloom in her eyes, I'd say she did. "It's okay. Just leave him be."

"She's way too good for an asshole like you." Jana picks up her purse and jacket off the floor.

Don't I know it. But they both leave me, Jana putting her arm around Paisley. I'm going to lose her, I just know it. But then again, I never did deserve her.

I watch the two of them walk away and I lean against the wall, letting my back slide down until my ass hits the floor.

My mama came outside where she found my dad and me still smoking his pack of cigarettes, not saying much to one another. We looked up when we heard her approach and I knew before she even spoke.

"There was too much bleeding. They couldn't get it to stop. Armen—"

I stood and walked away. I couldn't hear her speak those words. To confirm my biggest fear.

As I walked away, my mama's sobs echoed in the stillness of the night. I stared at the window of the waiting room glowing in the dark, knowing I'd ruined seven lives that night.

But worst of all, I had killed my best friend.

"There's the doctor," Saige says.

"I just got off the phone with his parents and they said it was okay to talk to you, Saige," an aging man in scrubs says.

The two of them shuffle away, but in doing so, they grow closer to where I'm still sitting against the wall. Great, I get to be here to hear the news right from the doctor's mouth.

"He's out of surgery and doing well. His season is over and the beginning of next season will depend on how he heals and how rehab goes, but all in all, he's a lucky man. I've seen these cases before and they don't always end this well."

"Thank you so much, doctor. When can I see him?"

Saige is happy. Everyone will be happy.

"He's just waking up. Maybe a half hour or so. I'll have a nurse come and get you."

"Thank you," she says and walks back into the waiting room, telling everyone the news.

I hear cheers ring out as people say how relieved they are.

I stand up from the floor and walk toward the red exit sign. If it wasn't for me, Aiden wouldn't be in this situation at all. I have nothing to celebrate.

CHAPTER 25

"Hockey players break hearts. You knew this."

Paisley

I knock on Maksim's door and there's no answer, so I ring the doorbell. I know he's home. I gave him all night to get himself out of this blame game.

Nadiya opens the door wearing her cap and gown.

"Well, you look awesome," I say. "A couple weeks, right?"

"Yes, I cannot wait. I had my grad photos done this morning. Our parents come in two weeks. Are you ready to meet your future in-laws?" She laughs. "Inessa is a tough one."

"Are you sure they aren't going to be your in-laws?"

She laughs again. "Never."

"Is he in his room?" My voice turns serious.

She nods.

"Has he been out of bed at all?"

She shakes her head and I catch sight of Jessie on the couch.

"Hey, Jessie." I wave. I ask Nadiya, "You heard about Aiden, right?"

"The news says he's going to be okay. Is that true?"

"Yeah, he's out for what's left of the season and maybe part of next, but Saige says he's doing great and is in good spirits. I wanted to see if Maksim wanted to go visit him."

As I step forward, Nadiya puts her hand on my wrist. "Losing Armen… he can't stop blaming himself. The wound is deep and it never healed."

I nod because I know. I've known since he told me the story about losing his best friend. And it's probably because of my background that I don't want Maksim to live with that guilt in his life anymore. I want him to be healthy, vibrant and carefree. Not to think he has to be everyone's protector and then blame himself when something inevitably goes wrong.

"I know." I pat her hand and venture down the hallway.

I open the door to Maksim's bedroom. His drapes are drawn and he's sprawled out on his stomach in bed.

Sitting on the edge, I place my hand on his back, running it up and down, then I trace his tattoos. "Hey, sleepyhead."

He groans and wraps an arm around my waist, sliding over on the mattress to get closer to me. My fingers roam his body and run through his hair.

When I overheard him talking to Jana and he mocked her for suggesting he loved me, I was hurt. But it's okay if he doesn't love me. We've only been dating a short while. I can't be upset about it, even if it stings because I know my feelings for him.

"Come into bed," he murmurs.

"I'm going to see Aiden and wondered if you wanted to come."

His body tenses and his arm goes limp. Rolling over, he turns his back to me. "I'm not going."

I had a feeling this might happen. Sometimes I hate that my education helps me predict people's responses after I get to know them. "You have to get up and visit your friend. Sulking is doing no good."

"Sulking?" He huffs, throws the covers off himself, and walks into his en suite naked.

Without shutting the door, he relieves himself then washes his hands before moving to his drawers to grab a pair of track shorts.

"You can shower. I'll wait," I say.

"I'm not showering because I'm not going anywhere." He sits on the edge of the bed, staring at the wall in front of him.

"I think it's time you talk to someone." I know last night I was all about letting him do his own thing, but after what happened with Aiden and how he's taking it, it's clear to me that Maksim needs to deal with his issues.

"I'm not talking to anyone. What's therapy gonna do for me?"

My back straightens. I'm annoyed that he keeps pissing all over my profession. "It does a lot of people good. It might give you some perspective."

"You have thousands of dollars in student loans that say you have to think that."

I stand. "You're not serious. I get the whole 'I'm Russian and we don't talk feelings' thing"—I do my best impersonation of him, which is pretty terrible—"but it's a real profession and therapy helps a lot of people. It doesn't mean you're weak if you're in therapy. Do you even know why I chose my profession? You've never bothered to ask me. Probably because you don't believe in it." I blow out a breath.

He says nothing.

"I went to therapy after my dad left us and all throughout college. It's what got me to the point that I don't have such horrible abandonment issues that I can't date you. I'm healthy and stable enough to embark on a relationship with a man who's in the spotlight and has women all over the world admiring him. Have I been jealous a few times? Sure. Sue me. But this is pretty extreme in comparison to a normal relationship. But without therapy, I wouldn't be who I am. I'd be some twisted up, bitter woman with no confidence to tell you what she really thinks, who would never trust a man."

I inhale deeply, my chest heaving, my eyes tingling from the tears that want to fall. "Would you like it if I downgraded your profession all the time? Said that all you do is hit people and act like a goon for a living?"

He stands. "You can say whatever you want." He digs into a drawer and puts on a T-shirt.

"*Ugh!*" I yell. "Why are you doing this? Why are you pushing me away? Why do you want to be this person?"

He turns around with accusation in his eyes. "What person? There's nothing wrong with protecting the ones you love. It's admirable in a lot of people's eyes."

"Not when you harbor this much guilt. Aiden is fine, and even if he wasn't, it's not your fault. Armen wasn't your fault. You need to release yourself of the responsibility of it all."

He shakes his head at me in disgust. "Jesus Christ, you have no idea what you're talking about."

"Why? Because I'm a stupid psychologist?"

"You always make me feel small. Like I can't handle my shit. It makes me feel weak." He punctuates his words by stabbing his finger into his chest while he speaks.

I stop for a moment and catch my breath because I don't want us to get into a bigger argument or say something we can't find our way back out of. I decide to go at it a different way.

"You didn't even tell me your parents want you to marry Nadiya," I say. "What does that have to do with protection?"

He runs his hand through his hair. "They look at me to take care of her. Trusted me after I killed their son. Now I say screw off, she can go back to Russia?"

Oh shit. This is so much worse than I thought. I sit on the bed, my legs losing all their strength. "Are you going to tell them no?"

"I don't know. Nadiya hasn't told them about Jessie yet. We have a few weeks until she graduates to decide."

My mouth drops open. "In your head, do you just think you'll marry Nadiya and all four of us will live here together? When either of your parents visit, we just swap partners and I sleep with Jessie and you sleep with Nadiya?"

He groans and lets his head fall back. "I don't know, okay? I haven't thought that far ahead."

I cannot believe this man. He's blinded by his need to protect everyone around him. I stand from the bed, unable to be in this room with him any longer. "Well, think about it. Think about living for yourself, Maksim. Be the protector of yourself for once."

"What do I have to protect?"

I soak in his words until I think I find a suitable answer. "Nothing, I guess. Since you don't love me, you clearly don't have to protect your heart. So, bye, Maksim. I wish you all the luck in the world." I walk toward the door. "And I mean that, because I do love you. I knew heartbreak was a risk when I got involved with you, but it's that love that makes me want the best for you. Have a great life."

I dig my colleague's card out of my purse and place it on his dresser, walk out, and shut the door. I leave my hand on the door handle for a moment, tears welling in my eyes. Because if he twists that door open and begs me to stay, I might not have the willpower to say no.

But then I let my hand fall away. I can't be with a man

who doesn't believe in me or what I do… a man who doesn't even love me like I love him.

I walk down the hallway. Nadiya and Jessie are there waiting for me.

"Everything okay?" Nadiya asks.

I wind my arms around Nadiya and pull her into a big hug. "Please look after him."

Jessie runs her hand down my back. "Don't leave. You guys are so good for one another."

I step back, sucking back the tears until I can be alone. "It's better this way, but it was nice while it lasted. Good luck, you two."

With one last hug, I walk out of Maksim's house, climb into my car, and weep for the future I thought we had together. I really did love him, even if I wasn't on his list of people to protect.

I drive over to Jana's as soon as I leave Maksim's.

She probably knew where all this was going after last night, so she opens the door with martinis in hand. I accept one and collapse into her arms, shedding more tears.

"I will kick his ass, you know that, right?" Her hand runs down my back.

I nod into her neck. We make it to her couch, and I lie with my head in her lap, her fingers running through my hair.

"Hockey players break hearts. You knew this, yet you fell in love anyway."

"He was so sweet. The stuff he said to me. I really thought he was different."

She sips her martini. "He didn't cheat on you, Paise. His head is just all messed up. It's still fixable."

I laugh because that is one bonus. At least I'm not the stupid woman who didn't know he was cheating on me.

"He'll probably have ten women in his bed tonight." I wail at the thought, invoking a fresh torrent of tears.

"He's not like that."

The television is on, so without bothering to ask Jana why she has ESPN on, I sit up and grab her remote to turn up the volume so I can find out what people are saying. "Langley apologized?"

"He went to the hospital last night after everyone left. Said he was sorry to Aiden, I guess. The press was there when he left, so he said he didn't want to make it a big deal, but he also doesn't want kids to get the wrong idea. That it's not how you play hockey and he's been so blinded by hate that he let his emotions get the best of him. He kind of alluded to Ford but didn't say his name outright."

I sit back and take a sip of the martini, cringing at the amount of olive juice in it. How does she drink these?

"He's sure got his head on straight," I say, wishing Maksim was the same.

"Yeah, makes those hormones go into a frenzy."

Not me though. Although it's admirable what Langley did, my hormones only respond to one hockey player now.

"You know something funny?" I say.

"What?"

"We didn't even do our nine dates. I fell in love with him in eight dates. That has to be a record."

I think back to all the dates we had. The candy place, Costco, then our latest date, where we built a blanket fort in his family room and binged Netflix all night, only for the fort to crash down when we were having sex.

"Just be happy you didn't waste your time with eighteen dates or something."

She's right, I should be thankful I didn't waste more time on Maksim. But what I really regret is allowing my heart to get involved, because right now, it feels as if it's going to take a lifetime to heal.

CHAPTER 26

"That's what flowers and apologies are made for."

Maksim

"You're an idiot," Nadiya says when I enter the kitchen a while later.

"Another reason why I'm happy I'm a lesbian," Jessie says.

I roll my eyes, ignoring them and walking out the patio door toward the beach. I hold on to the railing while I stretch. I'm not much of a runner, but jogging seems to clear everyone's heads in the movies and shit, so I'm gonna give it a try. I bring up one leg to stretch my quads.

"Seriously, she's perfect for you. What did you do?" Apparently Nadiya has followed me out.

Thankfully Jessie stayed inside.

"It's none of your business. She ended it." I switch legs.

"Oh no, you don't. You're not going to sit here and blame her. Because that girl who walked out of here wasn't a girl who wanted to end it. She might've been given no choice, but she didn't want it to end." Her finger's pointing at me and her voice is rising.

"Ne vmeshivaisya v eto, Nadiya," I say, bending to touch my toes.

"You are my business. The minute my brother chose you to be his best friend, that made you my business."

I roll my eyes again and stretch my arms over my head.

"Well, your brother is dead, so take me off your list of concerns."

Her hand lifts and I see it coming before I feel it. She slaps me across the face.

"*Poshol na hui*, Maksim. What do you think Armen would think of you right now? Screwing up your entire life. For what? Hell, he's probably your damn angel and brought that woman into your life. And you just chew her up and spit her out. For what? Because of what happened to Aiden? He's fine and what happened to him isn't your fault."

"So everyone keeps saying," I say, jogging in place.

She shakes her head. "I'm going to call your mama."

"Don't forget she wants you to be my wife. Are you gonna call her every time you're not happy with my husbandly performance?"

Her fists clench at her sides. "We're not getting married."

"Then tell your parents about Jessie."

She stares at me silently.

"What?" I inch forward. "Want me to mind my own business?"

She says nothing, so I continue to egg her on.

"Thought so."

Everyone talks a good game, but at the end of the day, it's still up to me to protect them when they can't do it for themselves.

I jog off the patio and onto the sand. Damn, this is harder than it looks. My feet keep sliding, so I go toward the water where the sand is packed down. I get in a good groove, hoping for clarity to come, but it doesn't. I'm still the same piece of shit who killed my best friend and got another best friend seriously injured.

I cut through a yard and walk five blocks to the nearest

bar, then find a vacant stool to sit my ass on. Option two for figuring out what the hell is wrong with me—alcohol. But two beers in and I'm annoyed by the stares from patrons and the few who interrupted my self-reflection by asking for an autograph, so I split.

The next day I'm chilling at my house, staring at the TV. Thankfully, Nadiya and Jessie are gone. I'm sick of their opinions. When the doorbell rings, I roll my eyes, wondering who's next up to give me advice.

Ford doesn't wait to be let in, just uses his key I gave him.

"Asshole," he says, helping himself into my fridge and grabbing Nadiya's leftover pizza.

"Please help yourself," I deadpan.

He sits in a chair and stares at me while I'm watching SportsCenter. We can pretty much chalk our season up to being done now that we've lost our top-line center.

"That's what best friends do," he says. "I know you and Aiden have some sort of bromance thing going on, but I like to think we're best friends too."

I shake my head at him.

"Otherwise, you wouldn't have given me a key."

"I gave you that key to check on the house three years ago when Nadiya and I went back to Russia. You never gave it back."

He ignores my comment. "So… why are we depressed and why is the pretty therapist moving everything out of her office at the Fury offices?" He sits back with the pizza on his lap. "I mean, I have problems, man, but you're causing your own problems."

"You caused your own too when you stuck your dick in someone you didn't know."

"Touché," he says, biting the piece of pizza.

I don't bother asking about Paisley. Her work is none of my business anymore now that she broke up with me. "I'm not depressed. And she broke up with me, so I have no idea why she's doing what she's doing."

He nods, lips pressed together. "Aiden said you haven't been by." His eyebrows raise.

He might be one of the only men I know who grooms himself to the point of having perfect eyebrows. And because we share a locker room, I know he does a perfect manscaping job too.

"I haven't had the time," I say.

"He's back home now. On bedrest. Poor guy can't even fuck until he's cleared of his concussion."

I nod. "I'm sorry to hear it."

"Then go visit the guy." He drops the box on the coffee table and stands. "Tell me Nadiya is on her period. It's the only time you have junk food around here and I'm dying for a Coke."

"I have no idea."

I used to mark it on the calendar, hoping it'd be when I was traveling. Living with a woman for the past four years has definitely prepared me for mood swings. But Nadiya found out and let's just say she didn't appreciate my efforts.

He comes back with a Coke, and I wonder momentarily if that's why Nadiya went off on me like she did. Doesn't matter because if I'd asked if she was on her period, she'd probably beat me to death with a bag of Oreos.

"Okay, I'm done with this. I don't like it. I need you to be the glue that keeps us all together." Ford's voice has a whine to it. "And I know I don't believe in monogamy, but you and the pretty therapist had something good going. I'm not blind. I knew you two were screwing. Especially in Nashville when that Russian beauty kissed you. I felt the wave of female pissed-offness from Paisley."

"It's over. She broke up with me. I told you that." I stand and grab my keys. "Let's go to Drake's."

I'd rather face embarrassment with him than sit around here and talk about Paisley all day. The only thing more painful than knowing I failed another friend is knowing I failed her.

"Cool." He scribbles a note on the empty pizza box and puts it back in the fridge.

Nadiya's going to murder him one day.

***

"Hey, he's been asking about you." Saige hugs me and kisses my cheek when she answers the door. "He's in the family room."

I walk through his house, saying a quick hello to Aiden's mom and sister. I've been to Wisconsin on more than one occasion, and they come down to Florida at least once a year, so we've met a bunch of times.

His nephews and niece are in the pool with his dad. I pop my head back there to say a quick hello before going over to Aiden and giving him a hug.

"Hey," I say.

"About time." Aiden knows me and he knows about Armen, so I'm pretty sure he's put two and two together.

"Sorry, I was busy."

"Pretty therapist dumped him," Ford says.

"What?" Saige must have killer hearing. She walks in with her hands on her hips. "Why?"

Ford runs his hand down my body. "Clearly because he's turned into a bump on a log. Who wants to date that?"

"Ford, my nephews need someone to throw them in the air in the pool. Saige, babe, give me and Maksim a minute," Aiden says.

"I'm not leaving. I'm sick of being cut out of shit. When my life was falling apart, we included you, Shamrock. We're a threesome." Ford crosses his arms and I laugh for the first time in two days.

"Fine. Stay, but if you say one thing about monogamy, I'm gonna have my triplet nephews punch you in the nuts," Aiden warns then sets his eyes on me. "Don't do this to yourself." He gestures to his arm in a sling. "This is not your fault. I'll heal and I'll be good. And this might be my first concussion that knocked me out, but it probably won't be my last. None of this is because you got ejected. Langley apologized, I accepted. I signed up for this when I signed up to be a professional hockey player."

"But my job—"

"Bullshit. You've taken the role of keeping us all safe for way too long. Your job out there is to prevent the opposing team from scoring. Sure, you need to protect us, but you've been taking cheap shots like you have to prove something out there."

"I can't speak for Aiden, but I have fun on game days. Can you say the same?" Ford chimes in.

"I love my job." They both quirk their eyebrows at me, so I say, "I guess over the years I've enjoyed it less and less."

"Since we all got close. Since we became—"

"A threesome," Ford says again.

"I was gonna say friends, but yeah." Aiden smiles at me.

"I guess." I shrug.

He's right though. Once I considered them my true

friends, I played more aggressively, ready to protect them no matter the repercussions.

"We're tough guys too, you know," Aiden says.

"Well, I do have the prettiest face out of the three of us," Ford says, beaming. "I'd hate for it to be beat up. The ladies might complain."

We both groan.

"What? I'm sorry, but you know I'm the pretty one." He looks at us like we can't possibly argue.

"Go win Paisley back. She's good for you," Aiden says.

"I said a lot I can't take back," I tell them.

"That's what flowers and apologies are made for," Ford says.

"It's gonna take a lot more than that." I sit and think about all the nasty things I said to her. How I lied when I said I didn't love her. When she said she loved me, all I wanted to do was bury my head in her neck and profess my love right back, but I couldn't get my feet or my mouth to move. She already thought I was a piece of shit, so why try to change her mind?

"Then do whatever it takes to get her back," Aiden says. "If you love her like I think you do, then you do whatever you can to win her over again."

"I've got this whole thing with Nadiya and my parents. I don't want Paisley in the middle of all that." Which is the truth. She deserves a lot better than a guy who won't stand up to his parents.

"She's gonna slip out of your grasp if you wait too long," Ford says.

"Let's just watch the game," I grumble.

Lucky for me, Aiden's triplet nephews run in and jump on Ford, ending the conversation.

"Hey, you're messing up my hair," he yells as they

climb all over him, laughing. "Who cuts your nails? Edward Scissorhands? Jeez. I'm gonna need stitches."

We all laugh, watching them ruin Ford's country club look.

"Best five dollars I ever spent." Aiden's dad comes in, putting his hand out in front of me. "Nice to see you, Maksim."

"You too." I shake his hand, swallowing the guilt I feel over failing to protect his son.

Maybe Paisley's right about one thing. Maybe it is time I live my life for myself.

Chapter 27

"I want to be someone you can be proud of."

Paisley

I walk into Mr. Gerhardt's office for the last time as someone who works for him.

"I'm leaving now," I say.

"I can't convince you to stay?" Mr. Gerhardt rises from his office chair.

"I don't think I'm meant to work here. If anyone needs me, send them to my main office."

It was a tough decision, but I signed off on everyone but Maksim. I just can't in good conscience allow him to skate out of therapy when he might be the one on the team who needs it the most. And that's saying a lot when his teammate is Ford.

"So… Maksim?" He lowers his chin and looks at me from under his bushy eyebrows.

"Jana told you." I can't even be mad at her at this point. I was terrified for the man in front of me to know, and now that he does, it feels very anticlimactic given the circumstances.

He nods. "But only after I questioned her after hearing about you two being the first ones at the hospital together. You could've told me. I feel like a fool that I kept setting you up."

"It's against the rules for me to be involved with a patient."

He laughs. "Oh, Paisley, my rule follower. I always knew my daughter picked the best friend. My wild child needs a girl like you to keep her in line. But sometimes rules are meant to be broken. Someone said that once."

I cringe. "Not when it comes to the ethics of my profession. But I did it anyway. My conscience tells me I never acted as his therapist though, so I guess that makes it a little better."

He looks over my shoulder, seeming to be thinking, then meets my gaze squarely and huffs. "When I first met Maksim, I wanted him on the Fury. A lot of teams felt the same way. With his size, he could be a big contributor. He was from Russia, and I think people assume Russians can be cold, cutthroat when they need to. Like they don't bleed or something. But Maksim bleeds, he feels. Doesn't he?"

Wetness coats my eyes when I think of what Maksim has endured. I nod, wiping my eyes with the backs of my hands.

"Oh, sweetheart." He comes around his desk, takes me by my upper arms, and pulls me in for a hug, more of a father to me than my own. "That's why I wanted him. I don't want some player with no emotion out there on the ice. I wanted a guy who could be part of a team, a good guy for the community. Maybe that's why I've been so hard on him this year, wanting him to straighten himself out. Maybe I pushed too hard."

I pull back. "I suggested he try therapy with a colleague of mine. Obviously you can do what you want since I didn't sign off, but it might help." I can't say much more than that without feeling as though I'm betraying Maksim's confidentiality.

He nods as though maybe he's familiar with Maksim's

story. "I appreciate everything. I know this didn't work out like we planned, but I think in the end, you coming here might have changed your life for the better."

I shake my head. "Maksim and I are done. It was nice while it lasted, but we're over."

He purses his lips. "Take it from an old man. Nothing is black and white. Always keep your heart open for a second chance."

"Thanks, Mr. Gerhardt. I better get going." I want to be out of here before the players come in for practice.

He kisses my cheek. "Come by for dinner soon."

"I will."

I leave his office and head to mine to grab the last box—only to find Maksim standing in the middle of the room. My heart betrays me and skips a beat because he looks almost happy.

"Maksim," I say, grabbing my box.

"Paisley, can I have a word?"

"No, I don't think so. I have to get going." I walk out of the office and he follows. "Please just leave me alone."

"I can't do that because we never had our ninth date."

"That's because we're not dating anymore. Did you forget we broke up?" I press the elevator button and purposely look away from him.

"Oh, I remember. I've been depressed over it for days until I figured out that I don't want to break up."

Ugh, anger makes my blood pressure rise. "How nice for you. Should I jump into your arms or let you fuck me in the elevator because you've decided you don't want our relationship to end? Screw you."

The elevator doors open, and he takes a step forward to follow me, but the maintenance guy is in it with a big trash receptacle and I've taken up all the available room. This couldn't be more perfect.

"Sorry, no room." I press the button to close the doors.

Maksim removes his hand when the doors don't stop from closing. Got to love mechanical difficulties when they work in your favor.

"Sorry," I say to the maintenance guy as we go down.

He shakes his head.

The elevator stops on the ground floor and I file out, heading to the parking lot. As I reach the doors, the emergency staircase door opens, and a breathless Maksim rushes out.

"Just listen to me."

I stop at the door and rest the box on my hip. "What?"

"I love you."

I give him a saccharine smile. "Nice. Bye."

I walk out of the Fury building, but of course he follows me, running and walking backward in front of me while he talks.

"I'm serious and I know that's not enough, but I'm going to do the work. I'm going to talk to someone. But I want to make sure you'll wait for me."

"You cannot be serious."

"Please, *kotik*," he says, and my last nerve sizzles and snaps.

"No!" I put up my finger. "Don't use that word for me. You lost the right when you laughed off the idea of ever loving me to Jana. When you said those mean things to me. So my name is Paisley Pearce to you now."

He bites the corner of his lip to stop from smiling.

God, I'd love to smack him across the face right now. "Stop laughing."

"I'm sorry. Paisley then." He holds up his hands. "I know you love me."

I reach my car and put the box on the hood, turning around. "You have no idea what I feel for you right now."

"You wouldn't be talking to me if you didn't. Plus, I know that the love we shared doesn't just go away. The connection we have doesn't disappear. Just wait for me. I promise I'm coming for you as soon as I have my head sorted out. I want to be someone you can be proud of."

Another round of tears hits my eyes and I almost give in. I almost crack and let him back in my life, but then I remember his words and a fresh wave of pain hits me. "I am proud of you. I was proud of you. What you endured is more than most people go through and you got through it. That's a testament to your strength and perseverance. But I put myself out there once and I got burned. I'm not sure I can do it again."

I step forward, placing my hand over his heart. I close my eyes for a moment to gain the strength to put the final ax in this cord tying us to one another because I never again want to feel what I am right now.

"I'm so happy you're going to get help, but don't do it for me or for us. Do it for yourself. There's no turning this thing between us around. I wish you the best of luck, Maksim." I rise up on my tiptoes and kiss him on the cheek. Then I grab my box, climb into my car, and start the engine.

"This isn't over. I'm not accepting no," he says to my closed window.

Without looking at him, I drive off, leaving him in my rearview mirror.

CHAPTER 28

"You look good, Maksim."

Maksim

I stand at the baggage claim with Nadiya. It's been two weeks since I last saw Paisley and I'm pissed off about it. I took her advice and called the guy on the card she left me. After only two visits, I'm feeling a little better, a little more myself. He said the fact that I admitted I was having problems dealing with the past was a great start.

"So where's Jessie?" I ask.

"I'm telling them first. I'm going to introduce them to her tonight if things go well."

Nadiya came to me last night and said she's going to tell her family about Jessie. She doesn't want to marry me just for a chance to stay here longer. I told her that was good because I couldn't have married her anyway, no matter how much I wish I could make the situation right for her. So we're going to a very public place to discuss this with our parents so they can't flip out on us.

Just then, our four parents come down the escalator, our moms laughing and our dads complaining about the custom lines, I'm sure. I can tell that Nadiya is nervous, so I take her hand and give it a quick squeeze. They spot us, and our moms have their arms open, walking toward us.

"*Nashi detki!*" they say.

I hug my mom, then we switch. I shake both of our dads' hands.

"You too thin, Nadiya," her mom says.

"Yes, too thin. You should feed her." My mom elbows me.

I shake my head. "She eats fine, Mama."

We get their baggage and climb into the SUV I rented for them to use while they're here.

"Oh, nice car, Maksim," Nadiya's mom says.

"It's just a rental."

"He drives a fancy sports car," Nadiya says.

My dad presses buttons on the dashboard. "Too hot. Make it colder."

I adjust the air conditioning, but when he figures out what to press, he turns it to max and high. I'm gonna freeze my nuts off.

"We're going to eat," I say to the group.

"Oh no, I cook you good Russian dinner," my mama says. "I brought all the stuff we need from the Russia in my suitcase."

I shake my head. She's lucky the guys in customs didn't know that. "We want to take you out."

"You don't want home cook meal from me?" My mama sounds as if she's on the verge of tears.

"Later. You're here for three weeks." *How will I ever get through three weeks?*

"Fine, but then we go to your house?" she asks.

"Da. We have big surprise," Nadiya's mom says.

"What is it?" Nadiya asks, meeting my eyes in the rearview mirror.

Both moms snicker, but they can't keep it in.

"I brought my wedding dress," Nadiya's mom says.

"How long until the restaurant?" Nadiya asks, sounding a little panicked.

I stop at a red light. "Fifteen minutes."

"We think instead of you coming back to Russia to get married, you marry here. Maksim, you can pull strings so it happens while we're here, right?"

"Sure, I know everyone in the government. I'm sure they'll bend the rules for me." I roll my eyes as Nadiya stares out the window.

I valet at the restaurant, which my parents think is ridiculous.

"We healthy. We can walk," my dad says.

"You mean your legs aren't freezing? Because I can barely walk." I shiver from driving in a deep freezer the entire way here. I tip the driver and take my number. "It's easier this way."

We sit at the reserved table in a seafood restaurant. I'm thankful we have some people around us who will hopefully keep our parents in check when we tell them the news about our plan not to marry. I feel bad for Nadiya. I'm not sure how her parents will take the fact that she's a lesbian. But I know they love their daughter, so my hopes are high.

We order drinks and appetizers, but I'm told those will just make me full, so I end up canceling them although I really wanted to try that crab cake.

"How you both doing?" my dad asks while checking prices on the menu. He's adding up what this will cost, I'm sure.

"I got the bill," I tell him. "Order whatever you want."

"You need to save your money," Mama says. "For babies." She looks at Nadiya as though she's hoping there's a baby in there already.

Why are they acting as if we've fallen in love?

"You do understand that I don't love Nadiya in a romantic way, right?" The sentence leaves my mouth without me thinking it through. I think it's because I want to stick up for Paisley even though she's not part of my life right now.

"What?" Her mom leans back in her chair, looking affronted.

"We're friends. If we marry—spoiler alert: probably not going to happen—we're not in love, which means we're not going to sleep together, which means no babies."

Both our mamas frown and look at one another. I can see they've been planning this for months without our input. I glance at Nadiya because she needs to finish this, but she says nothing.

All four sets of eyes are on us as though they don't understand.

"Maksim is in love with someone else!" Nadiya says, and they all gasp.

"And so is Nadiya!" I say back like true siblings.

They all gasp again.

The waiter comes over and I shake my head for him to come back.

"You in love?" my mama asks.

"He blew it though, Inessa." Nadiya opens up her fat mouth.

"You in love too?" her mama asks, and Nadiya nods. She pats Nadiya's hand. "Then you marry him. He American citizen?"

I disregard my mama's stare and look at Nadiya. Reaching under the table, I grab her hand and squeeze. If Nadiya wants to lie and make up a story about some man in her life, I'll go with it. I'm here to support her whether she's ready to come out to her family or not.

"I'm in love with a woman, Mama," she says quietly.

"Oh." Her mom slides back in her seat.

The table is quiet for a minute, so I jump in. "She's

really great. Her name is Jessie and she loves Nadiya so much. They're a great couple."

"What did she say? Woman?" her dad asks.

Her mom nods. "You're a lesbian?"

Nadiya nods. "Yeah, Mama."

Her mom and dad look at one another, almost having a silent conversation between them, then her mom grabs Nadiya's hand. "Is she citizen?"

Nadiya chuckles. "Mama, I'm not going to marry her."

But as she says that, Jessie comes toward the table with flowers in her hand.

This is why she wanted to know where I made reservations. I smile at Jessie. Way to go.

Nadiya tears up, and our parents watch as Jessie falls to her knee, opens up a ring box and asks Nadiya to be her wife. I release her hand from under the table. Nadiya slides out, falling to the floor, and accepts through her tears.

Our parents are looking around as if they're just barely understanding what's happening.

"This is Jessie." Nadiya holds Jessie's hand and presents her to the table.

Jessie hands the flowers to Nadiya's mom.

My dad looks up from the menu and looks at my mom. "Who she?"

"Nadiya's fiancée." My mama smiles.

It's then I take an easy breath for the first time in a long time. I'm no longer responsible for Nadiya. The weight I've been carrying around lifts from my shoulders, and I feel lighter than I have in years.

*A*fter my parents are comfortable at my house and Jessie and Nadiya are talking wedding plans, I say I have to run out for an errand, but I drive by Paisley's office.

Her light is on, and I sit in the dark SUV she's not familiar with and watch her like a creepy Peeping Tom. Her hair is pinned up and she looks as if she's closing up for the day. My body yearns to go to her. It's begging to feel her under me, to be buried deep inside her softness. I miss the way she hugged me or just rested her forehead on mine and said hello as though it was the best part of her day.

She comes out of the building and glances over. Our eyes lock for a moment. She lifts her finger and puts her stuff in her car, then she crosses traffic and comes to my side of the car on the curb.

"I saw Instagram. Please tell Nadiya and Jessie I say congratulations."

"It was kind of crazy. Jessie's got a set of nonexistent balls, that's for sure."

She laughs and it's like a knife in the chest because I miss that sound.

"I guess you're off the hook, huh?" She smiles, but not in a relieved way. She looks genuinely happy for me.

I nod. Did two weeks apart really get us to acting as if we're acquaintances? As if we've only ever been friends and not each other's everything at one point?

"Yeah. And it felt good. To know that I'm not responsible for her."

Her hand runs down my forearm. "You never were. I have to get going, but please tell them both congratulations from me. I'll send a gift."

I nod. "I'll tell them."

"You look good, Maksim," she says, her dimples showing.

"So do you." I want to say so much more, but I'm only two weeks into therapy. Hardly long enough that she'd think it had made a difference.

She crosses the street, slides into her car, and gives me one last wave before she drives off. I sit there and wait for her taillights to disappear, wishing like hell she was right next to me.

CHAPTER 29

"Ya lublu tebya."

Paisley

Two weeks after my last Maksim Petrov sighting, I prepare myself to see him tonight.

Nadiya and Jessie are getting married and they invited me. I was going to decline, but there are a lot of working parts when it comes to Maksim and me. We have mutual friends and are bound to see one another at parties. Might as well bite the bullet. Plus, I can't deny being curious about his parents and this may be my only opportunity to see them.

At the wedding, I slip off my shoes and put them in the basket, stepping into the sand. There aren't many chairs, which makes me happy that I accepted the invitation. It doesn't look as though a lot of people were invited.

I catch sight of Aiden and Saige talking to an older couple. Saige sees me and waves me over, but she excuses herself and meets me halfway.

"You look gorgeous," she says, hugging me. "I'm so happy you came."

I smile. "I'm nauseous and scared to death."

She laughs and I do too.

"You came," Maksim says behind me.

I close my eyes and release a deep breath before turning around.

"I'll leave you two to talk," Saige says and walks back over to Aiden.

Our eyes take in one another for a moment. He's so much taller when I'm not wearing shoes. I want to step into him, feel him, smell him, let him hold me.

"Hey," he says after a moment.

"Hi."

And we're back to staring at one another.

"Maksim," a woman calls from his patio. "She's here."

He looks back. "I'm sorry. I gotta go." He leans forward and his hand on my waist feels as though it sears my skin when he kisses my cheek. "You look stunning as always."

Then he's gone and I can't tell him that he looks handsome in his khakis and white shirt. There are a million things I want to tell him. I'm sorry his season is over. That he played some great last games. That I can tell he's enjoying playing more than ever before.

I find Saige and sit down beside her, saying hello to Aiden and waiting for the ceremony to start. Candles lit in vases are placed in a row down the walkway to the flower-covered arbor.

"Pretty therapist," Ford says and sits down on my other side.

"Hey, Ford," I say.

"You could reciprocate with handsome hockey player." He elbows me. "But I get it, you only think one hockey player is handsome, right? I mean, I wouldn't want my girl going around and complimenting other players."

"I'm not Maksim's."

He gives me a look. "You'll always be Maksim's."

I open my mouth to say something, and he raises his eyebrows as though challenging me to say differently, so I shut my mouth. Because he's right. I'll always be Maksim's.

The music starts, and Jessie and her parents walk down the aisle. The woman who called Maksim from the porch walks down with who I presume is her husband.

Then the music changes, and we all turn to find Maksim at Nadiya's side at the end of the makeshift aisle. He winks at me and tears well in my eyes. He looks at the sky for a moment, whispering something, then smiles at Nadiya, and they walk down between the rows of chairs.

The ceremony is beautiful and happens just as the sun is setting. Watching a couple commit to a life together does something to me. Makes me believe in fairy tales and happily ever afters. By the time they seal their marriage with a kiss, Saige and I are both messes.

Sparklers are given to everyone instead of bubbles or birdseed, and we all have fun with them. Ford almost lights my dress on fire by accident, but I laugh it off.

The happy couple thanks everyone for coming and tell us there's a buffet inside Maksim's house. I can't bear to go in when the house reminds me so much of us, so I remain outside, drinking on the beach.

"I thought you might want to eat something." Maksim hands me a plate and sits down next to me on the sand.

Nadiya and Jessie are dancing, as well as some of their friends.

"They're beautiful together," I say.

"Yeah, now I have to deal with both sets of our parents on my own for a week since they're going on their honeymoon."

I laugh. "At least it all worked out."

"Not all of it."

My heart skips.

"I don't have you." His voice is low and serious.

"Maksim," I say, shaking my head. "Not here. Not now."

A woman I saw earlier who resembles Maksim comes over to us. "You're her."

"*Ne seichas*, Mama," he says.

"You're the one he loves." She shoos her son away. "Go, Maksim. I need a word."

"Mama," he says again.

"Go." Her tone brooks no argument and my eyes widen.

He listens and shoots me a look of apology before stepping away.

"I'm Inessa, his mama."

I hold out my hand. "Paisley."

"I want to thank you. You pulled my boy out of the darkness."

I shake my head. "No, I didn't have anything to do with that."

"You did. He told me. He's going to therapy. We talked the other night until the stars went to sleep. He said he didn't know what was wrong until you came into his life. He wants to be better for you."

"That's kind, but you're giving me too much credit."

She rests her hand on my knee. "I saw when you walked in. Your back was to him, but he stared for the longest time before he could be strong to approach you. Even now, he's not sure how to act, but a mama knows and I see it in his eyes. He loves you."

"I—"

She holds up her hand. "Why do you young people make love so complicated? You love him. He loves you. That is enough. Love is enough. I'm married thirty-five years. Love is what gets you through."

I smile at her advice.

"I don't know what happened. But I know what I see. What my son has told me. How he talks about you and what a fool he was to let you go. If you feel the same, why spend this time apart?"

In the distance, I see Nadiya's mom getting out some Chinese sky lanterns.

Inessa looks at her and back at me. "If you want to put everything behind you and be together, light a lantern with Maksim. Let the wind take your problems away. Start over if you need to, but don't let the love you share fade away. Sometimes it only comes around once." She pats my knee.

"Thank you," I say.

She shrugs and smiles before walking over to Nadiya's mom.

As they pass around the Chinese sky lanterns, Maksim brings one over to my side. "Do you know how to light these and get it up?"

"Maksim," I say.

He's trying to pull it up and looking at where it needs to be lit. "Uh, huh?"

"Look at me."

He looks over. "I'm sorry about my mama. Whatever she said."

I shake my head. "You never took me on that ninth date."

The lantern slips out of his grasp, but he catches it before it hits the sand.

I laugh. "So…"

He swallows hard. "Why are you mentioning that?"

"Well, I was trying to be smooth."

He smiles. "Are you saying what I think you are?"

I nod.

He drops the lantern and takes me in his arms, picking me up off the sand. I laugh into his neck.

"*Ya lublu tebya.* I love you, Paisley. You know that, right? I love you so much and I'm so sorry for everything that happened and everything I said. I'm going to therapy, and you were right, it's helped."

"I know and I love you too, but, Maksim?"

He lowers me to the ground, his hands cradling my face. "What is it?" He stares me in the eye, his bright blues full of love.

"It's *kotik*," I say and he laughs, pressing his lips to mine.

Ten minutes later, we light a Chinese lantern, each of us holding one side before letting the wind take it, along with all our problems, and hope for some good luck for the future. But regardless, Inessa is right. For us, love is enough.

EPILOGUE

"Ask me again."

Maksim
START OF THE NEXT SEASON

"*I* was really starting to enjoy the off-season," Paisley says, rolling over in bed.

My hand ventures under the sheet and between her legs, gliding along her wetness. "I know, but just think, now you get to sit in the wife and girlfriend section. Everyone will know I belong to you."

She flips over and opens her arms for me to lie on top of her. "I thought it was me belonging to you."

"It's a mutual thing. Regardless, I'm taken."

"Yes, you are."

"So it's enough for you that we just live together? No symbolism?" I ask, wedging her legs open with my thighs.

"Of course it is."

"I wish I could say the same." I get up on my knees, bringing out the ring box that was under my pillow and opening it. "Will you make this permanent and be my wife? Spend your life with me?"

Her mouth drops open and she blinks a few times before she speaks. "You're proposing to me naked in bed? Right before you were about to push into me?"

"Paise, you're kind of killing the mood. It's a yes or no question."

I don't really care that she's talking about being naked

or anything else. I just want her to answer the question before my heart beats out of my chest from the anxiety this entire process had caused me.

Ring shopping with Ford was a bad idea. The man has Harry Winston taste with a Harry Winston wallet and wanted me to spend Harry Winston money. I wanted the best ring I could afford, but I want to be able to take care of my woman too.

Three carats isn't bad though. At least I hope not.

"Do you actually think I'd say no?" she asks, still not giving me a clear answer. "Oh, it's beautiful. Can I take it out?"

I snap the box shut and she retracts her fingers. "Only if you say yes."

"So you think I'd decline an offer to marry you?"

"Paisley," I bite out, and she laughs.

"You're so easy. You know that?"

"Answer the question before I return the damn thing."

"Return it?" Her mouth falls open. "You don't want to be one of those guys."

I drill my gaze into her. "This is a proposal. You're supposed to cry and fawn over the ring and plaster yourself to my body."

"I'm sorry." She sulks for a moment. "Ask me again."

I open the box. "Will you marry me?"

"Yes! Oh my god, I'm crying." She fans her face where there are no tears, then she throws herself on me, making me lose my balance and we fall to the floor with a thud.

"I guess we'll remember this moment forever."

She climbs on top of me, opens the ring box, puts the diamond on her left ring finger, and holds it up for me. "How do I look as Mrs. Petrov?"

"You look damn good, especially when you're only wearing the ring."

"Then show Mrs. Petrov what she's getting for the rest of her life."

I stand, lift her, and toss her on the bed. Falling to my knees, I grab her legs and yank her to the edge of the bed, swinging her ankles over my shoulders.

Five minutes later, she's screaming the three-letter word I was looking for, over and over again.

"*Y*ou have some spit-up right there." I point at Ford's jersey. He doesn't but I still enjoy busting his balls.

We're in the locker room for the first game of the season. He's been on baby duty most of the off-season. He and the baby mama have been trying this co-parenting thing, and it's worked out surprisingly well.

"Har har, just wait until you assholes get one," he says.

"Have one, you mean?" Aiden asks.

"Whatever, the thing cries all the time."

Sweet Annabelle Jacobs wailed her way into this world right after Paisley and I got back together, meaning Ford couldn't spend his off-season gallivanting around Europe with French models. Poor bastard. Or so he'd have you think.

"She, you mean," Aiden corrects him again, and I laugh.

"I love my daughter. I mean, I think I have that feeling dads talk about. I cried when she was born. That means something, right?" Ford asks us, as if either of us would know.

I'm not used to anything going normally—just look at my proposal to Paisley earlier. Not that I would change it. It's us and I love us.

"I'm surprised. You've manned up," I say, patting Ford on the back.

My phone dings in my locker.

"Let me guess, your leash is too taut and the master is calling." Ford rolls his eyes.

"Saige wants to throw you an engagement party," Aiden says to me.

"I bet Paisley would like that." I pick up my phone and blink. "Uh…" I read the message again.

"Hey, I have a great idea. My little one can be your flower girl if you wait a few years." Ford points at both of us. "She can do you both."

"Might want to rephrase that," Aiden says, shaking his head.

My phone dings again as another message comes through.

"What does the pretty therapist want?" Ford asks me. Clearly we're ruining the first game for him so far.

He's receiving an award for a scoring milestone before the game starts tonight. His baby mama, Britney, is supposed to bring Annabelle so Ford can show her off during the ceremony.

"She said Britney just got to the arena."

"Thank God she's on time. We had a talk about that earlier today. Half the time she's not showered when I get over there to pick up Annabelle and she's a hot mess."

"Well, she had a baby a few months ago," Aiden says. "Cut her some slack."

"Britney's not here anymore," I say. "Paisley says she dropped off the baby with her and took off. She said there's a note in the bag."

I look at Ford, whose mouth is hanging open. "What the fuck? She just left my kid with someone? No offense to Paisley."

"Want her to bring Annabelle down here with the note?" I ask, unsure of what to do in this situation.

"No. I gotta finish getting ready for the game."

"Ford," Aiden sighs.

"Just ask the girls to watch Annabelle until the game, okay? I'll get the note when they bring her down to the ice when I get the award."

He sits down, and I glance at Aiden, unsure what to do.

A half hour later, Paisley hands Ford Annabelle by the ice, he gets his award, pictures are taken, and he hands his baby back to Paisley while she hands him the letter. While the staff gets the carpets off the ice and gets it ready for us to skate, he opens the letter with Aiden and me on either side of him.

I'm really sorry, Ford. I can't do this. I'm not meant to be a mother. You're so good to her. Love her extra for me.

Britney

My eyes widen at Aiden and his mouth hangs open. Ford turns around, all the color drained from his face.

I pat him on the shoulder. "We'll be there for you. Whatever you need."

"I'm a single dad now?"

This is not good.

The End

Cockamamie Unicorn Ramblings

Man… this book took so long to write. We had two deadlines, and even on the last one we were worried we wouldn't hit it. Maksim and Paisley were hard nuts to crack, but in the end we found them.

There was going to be more of an enemies-to-lovers vibe in this book, but Maksim just knew Paisley was the one for him. When we title our books to get them up for pre-order we have a general outline of what the book will be about, but so many times when it comes time to write things don't turn out how we originally planned. Characters don't cooperate, we get a different/better idea as the series progresses, or what we originally wanted to do no longer feels right… which you know if you ever read our ramblings before. LOL

This book was no different but honestly, we don't remember what was supposed to be in this book. In the end they both just kind of fell on the page and we explored them through their journey until the emotional end. That was kind of a surprise, neither one of us saw how emotional the ending to their story would be.

Without our team you wouldn't have any of our books! Seriously, they take on a lot of the work off our hands so that we can write!

Andie Edwards – who was our Russian language/culture guru. This would have been impossible to pull off without you. Thank you so much for going above and beyond to assist us with this one!

Danielle Sanchez and the entire Wildfire Marketing Solutions team.

Cassie from Joy Editing for line edits.

Ellie from My Brother's Editor for line edits.

My Brother's Editor for proofreading.

Hang Le for the cover and branding for the entire series. Those colors!

Wander Aguiar for the inspiration of Maksim. Those eyes!

Bloggers who consistently carve out time to read, review and/or promote our work.

Piper Rayne Unicorns who love our characters like as much as we do! Thank you!

Readers who took the time to read our story when there's so many choices out there.

We can't tell you how excited we are for Ford's book. Who doesn't love a single dad in need of redemption? This one is a must read!

xo,

Piper & Rayne

About Piper & Rayne

Piper Rayne is a USA Today Bestselling Author duo who write "heartwarming humor with a side of sizzle" about families, whether that be blood or found. They both have e-readers full of one-clickable books, they're married to husbands who drive them to drink, and they're both chauffeurs to their kids. Most of all, they love hot heroes and quirky heroines who make them laugh, and they hope you do, too!

Also by Piper Rayne

Hockey Hotties

My Lucky #13

The Trouble with #9

Faking it with #41

Sneaking around with #34

Second Shot with #76

Offside with #55

Kingsmen Football Stars

You had your chance, Lee Burrows

You can't kiss the Nanny, Brady Banks

Over my Brother's Dead Body, Chase Andrews

The Baileys

Lessons from a One-Night Stand

Advice from a Jilted Bride

Birth of a Baby Daddy

Operation Bailey Wedding (Novella)

Falling for My Brother's Best Friend

Demise of a Self-Centered Playboy

Confessions of a Naughty Nanny

Operation Bailey Babies (Novella)

Secrets of the World's Worst Matchmaker

Winning My Best Friend's Girl

Rules for Dating your Ex

Operation Bailey Birthday (Novella)

The Greenes

My Beautiful Neighbor

My Almost Ex

My Vegas Groom

The Greene Family Summer Bash

My Sister's Flirty Friend

My Unexpected Surprise

My Famous Frenemy

The Greene Family Vacation

My Scorned Best Friend

My Fake Fiancé

My Brother's Forbidden Friend

The Modern Love World

Charmed by the Bartender

Hooked by the Boxer

Mad about the Banker

The Single Dad's Club

Real Deal

Dirty Talker

Sexy Beast

Hollywood Hearts

Mister Mom

Animal Attraction

Domestic Bliss

Bedroom Games

Cold as Ice

On Thin Ice

Break the Ice

Box Set

Charity Case

Manic Monday

Afternoon Delight

Happy Hour

Blue Collar Brothers

Flirting with Fire

Crushing on the Cop

Engaged to the EMT

White Collar Brothers

Sexy Filthy Boss

Dirty Flirty Enemy

Wild Steamy Hook-up

The Rooftop Crew

My Bestie's Ex

A Royal Mistake

The Rival Roomies

Our Star-Crossed Kiss

The Do-Over

A Co-Workers Crush